Gulfside Inn

A HAVEN BEACH NOVEL

REBECCA REGNIER

One

FAYE

To say Faye had a lot on her mind was an understatement. Her son was failing at OSU, and her sisters were at odds over an inheritance. Word had come down from management that layoffs were about to happen at the plant. And at that very moment, just as she was about to exit her Jeep, gazing in the rearview mirror, she realized a chin hair had escaped her notice for what appeared to be years and years.

It was long, and worse, it was white!

"How in the heck did you survive?"

Faye knew that the only way to find those suckers and pluck them effectively was in the car rearview. She was obsessed with making sure she got them. But somehow, this one made her look like a combination of Mrs. Claus and her 8th-grade English teacher. She didn't remember much about diagramming a sentence, but she did remember one thing. Mrs. Crabapple Did. Not. Care.

Faye cared. She found her tweezers and yanked it out with malice.

"Take that, you son of a gun." She directed negative energy to the follicle in hopes it got the picture. If you could manifest your dreams and aspirations, she was manifesting that her chin hairs withered into a quick and permanent death.

"And STAY out." Faye talked to her plants and seeds to encourage them to grow; it couldn't hurt to tell this chin hair it was unwanted, unloved, and should stay plucked.

She smoothed her index finger over her chin, tilting her head back and forth, assuring herself that it was just the one stray white hair. A knock on her Jeep window had her jumping in her seat.

"Jeez, Shawn! You scared me."

"Sorry."

Shawn Briggs was on the crew she supervised. He liked to give her all the gossip, which was nice since, moving up the ranks at the plant, she was supposed to stay above the fray.

Gossip at an auto plant was a soap opera no different than gossip at high school or a beauty salon. Even though the plant demographic was mostly men, they spread the word of affairs, jealousies, windfalls, and downfalls with as much fervent and florid detail as any manicurist worth her cuticle trimmer.

"Well," Shawn said, holding Faye's door open, "they're coming down today. The numbers say we're going to get hit hard."

Faye grabbed her lunch bag and slid out into the biting winter wind. Bad news flew on frigid air, and it moved fast.

People weren't buying the new high-end SUV. And even though they made the more affordable version SUV in Toledo, their plant was going to feel the pain.

Faye had been through layoffs. But mostly, in her career, she'd been through "mandatory" overtime assignments.

Her dad knew tougher times, from recessions to downturns. Mostly, she'd been able to work work work. And she never said no to work. As a single mom, as the daughter of local UAW brass

Bruce Kelly, and as a woman making cars, she prided herself on being tough, never calling off, and always saying yes, I'll take that shift.

Which all added up to the realization that she wasn't that worried. Layoffs were tough, but they had funds to support their brothers and sisters. She'd be there for her co-workers. That was drilled into her from an early age.

Shawn Briggs was new, young, and had zero seniority. She reminded herself that he and the rest of the team were probably scared. Faye would reassure them. She would be a steady presence. She'd help simmer down that pot of boiling rumor stew.

"Yeah, and so then Robbie spouts off about Carrie hanging with him over Little Sheba's." Shawn was now focused on in-plant romances instead of impending layoffs.

Okay, well, denial is a river in Toledo, apparently.

"Sorry, Shawn, I realize this is potentially the end of Carrie and Troy's epic love story, but I need to pop into the office before I head out to the floor."

"Yeah, yeah, okay, but do you think I'm out?"

Faye stopped; Shawn was barely older than her own son. He probably was out. Zero seniority. She tried to break it softly.

"You may be, but look, they bring people back all the time, and you'll get job counseling. It's better now than if you had a wife and kids. We'll all get you through this. Okay?"

Shawn had stopped talking gossip. He was skinny and tall, and when he swallowed, you could see his Adam's apple bob up and down. He took a breath.

"Okay, thanks, Faye. You're right. My uncle said I should be an electrician. Maybe I should switch gears."

"Sure, see it as an opportunity. Catch you later." A few encouraging words: yes, holding his hand, no. She heard her dad in her ear, get on with it, kid. Get to bouncing back!

Shawn nodded and headed into the massive structure that was the auto plant. Faye went the opposite way, walking to the offices.

Most days she tried to avoid the offices, but she had this email. She'd likely get the corporate line on how to manage her staff, with the pending reductions.

Terry Fielder was the manager on duty. The suit as they were known. That was a term for management in a bygone era. They didn't wear suits anymore. They wore annoying logoed polo shirts. She missed the suits. It was easier to tell who was who when she first started almost thirty years ago. They ought to call them quarter zips or the khakis. She chuckled to herself at that idea.

"Faye, good to see you. Thanks for coming up."

"Sure, I don't have much time, though. They're jumpy on the floor, as you can imagine. I need to calm 'em down. We've all been through this before."

"About that, yes. Really. Sit." Terry was ten years younger than Faye, mid-thirties. But he made up for his lack of experience with bluster and corporate cliches. He was the first to "stick a pin in things," to "circle back," and use words like "synergy." She tried not to roll her eyes. They must learn that lingo in middle management school.

He saw himself as a boss and Faye and her line workers as beneath him. Even though she knew, with overtime, she outearned the heck out of this guy. Whatever, she didn't really need to work with Terry. Their interactions were minimal if her crew hit their targets, which they always did.

"As you know, we're tasked with twenty percent, and this is going to be hard on me, for sure, doing this, but from your section, we're talking, uh, let's look at the numbers." Terry didn't look at Faye. He looked at his computer screen and continued to bloviate. "Tasked," that was another one. You used to complete a task, but now you were tasked.

"So, yes, you'll be reduced by two dozen."

"That's over half my crew. You said twenty percent, not fifty."

"No, yes, sure, but we're getting leaner, more efficient, redundancy is the concern. And it is twenty percent total, of which..."

"I'm not running a redundant shift," she interrupted Terry, "and we're busy. We're asked to work weekends. How in the heck is that not efficient?"

Terry kept typing and looking at his computer screen as if the answer was there. Faye knew he had zero power, and he was told what to do and how to do it. Her co-workers were percentages on his screen, numbers that represented Shawn or Walter or Cassie.

"Honestly, you're at the high end of the pay scale. Corporate is doing seniority, of course, but that's also what I wanted to offer you."

She was a senior worker; at 48, she was one of the old guys now.

"Offer me?"

"Yes, you'll be transferring to the Warren, Michigan plant. We can't keep you on the books here, so they're laying off their fore-man, and you'll be needed there."

"Wait, what? Warren? I've been here nearly thirty years! Warren is over an hour's commute. How is seniority factoring in when I'd have to commute so far away?"

Terry stopped typing. Faye was mad, and her voice revealed it. She tried to be cool and calm, but they were asking her—no, *telling* her—to take a job in another town, in another plant, with people she didn't know from Adam.

"You're a valuable member of the team, but..."

"But you're farming me out instead of asking me what works for the crew here and for my own life?"

"I don't...We don't..." Terry didn't finish either sentence.

"I don't want to work in Warren." Her life was here, her house. Her son, when he wasn't at OSU, made Toledo his homebase. OSU was two hours away; Warren would be three. What was Terry even saying?

"Well, there's one more option." Terry went back to his computer and started typing again.

Faye felt unmoored. Someone had taken the rope off the post

and pushed her little boat into the choppy lake. She had no oars, no motor, no direction. Warren? Her house here was paid off. She had her garden. Three hours a day on the road if she commuted to Warren. Was this the way they rewarded loyalty? You had no choice. You just had to accept it, or what? Be laid off?

It's all because someone else decided on a number. Someone who never met her or saw that her attendance was perfect. Someone in some office far away who couldn't appreciate that she was great at keeping her crew efficient and happy in their roles. Or understand that the history of the place was also in her, as well as the future.

Or maybe not the future. She wasn't the future of this place at all. Not anymore.

Faye wished she could talk with her dad right now. Bruce Kelly would know how to handle this, what to say to the "suits." But he was gone. Most of his buddies were, too.

"Okay, I need to confirm with HR, but you're just under thirty in. Normally, you need to be over fifty for this, but you have over twenty years in, which means we can offer a buyout."

"What?" Faye had a hard time understanding what Terry was saying.

"Yeah, you can do early retirement. I'll get HR to work up the package. If you don't want to go to Warren."

Faye sat there; she had no idea what the buyout would look like. Could she afford to retire? At her age? What about health insurance for her son and his tuition? She'd always worked. Retire?

She only knew one thing. She didn't want to go to Warren. She wasn't going to start over at this company in a strange town. Nope. Not doing it. She decided on the spot, heck no, she won't go.

"I'm not going to Warren. Send me the offer."

"Will do. I'll circle back around on—"

"—Circle back around on *this*. I'm going down to the floor and let my crew know. Not for you, but for them. This is going to be rough."

"I've got a list of talking points for you to convey."

Faye leveled a stare at Terry. She didn't know what it looked like on his side of the desk. But from behind her eyes, it was a laser-beam-eyeballs-burning-the-computer-down situation.

"Right, you'll say the right thing."

Terry stood up, too, and smoothed his hands over his khaki pants. Faye turned and walked out of the office.

No matter what the offer, she was done here. She'd make sure her team knew the resources available to them.

But that was it. Thirty years. And she was done.

She'd packed her last lunch. She'd punched her last timecard.

Which was terrifying. But also liberating.

Except for that college tuition thing...

Ugh, that buyout package better be good.

Two

ALI

Water. It was the lure and the bane of Ali's existence right now. She'd sealed the roof. But the water was still there. She'd recalked the window frame, but the leak continued.

"Where are you coming from?"

Ali looked out the window of the Mango Mansion. The question was ridiculous. Outside that window was the entire Atlantic Ocean. Where was the water coming from? Ha. Where *wasn't* it coming from?

Ali looked around the cottage. She'd done a lot in a little time. She'd repainted the bedrooms, she'd replaced the appliances in the kitchen, and she'd even put down luxury vinyl plank flooring in that same little kitchen. There was not an inch she hadn't touched in the Mango Mansion, but still, the moldy smell.

Ugh.

She had a few days to solve the mystery of the Mango Mansion mold before she was supposed to open its doors to guests. Moldy

Mango did not have the same ring on a brochure. She'd have to solve this issue fast.

Despite the continued battle with this unit, Ali did feel hope. She had bookings for two of the six cottages for the peak week of spring break.

This was progress. She was feeling confident enough to insist on Didi and Jorge taking the week off. They'd be back to help her when the guests arrived, but this week, they were visiting their grandchildren in Atlanta. Ali was happy about that. Didi and Jorge were important to her and to The Sea Turtle, but they were in their seventies. They deserved a little rest. And every day they took off, Jorge seemed a little stronger.

Ali felt at home but also a stranger in a strange land all at the same time.

After almost two months of work on the cottages, she knew where most things were stored in the office. She'd set up a new booking system, taking The Sea Turtle from pencil and paper logs that Didi favored into the 21st-century computer era.

She knew Moe's Grocery had the best whole chickens on Wednesday, and she knew no matter how hot she got working on fixing the Mango Mansion up for the coming spring break season, she could take a dip in the ocean and feel brand-new again.

It gave her a little perverse glee to know that, back in Toledo, the school was closed due to "dangerous cold."

That fact was a revelation. Every day Ali spent living on the ocean, the cells of her body felt like they were reconstituting. It was as if the sea, air, and saltwater were part of her, but somehow, she'd been without them for most of her life. And now that she was right here, she was where she was supposed to be. Not that life was perfect; she had a divorce pending, a mystery unsolved about how her mother had come to own this place and then leave it to her, and then there were her two sisters. If she messed this up...

Ali had no one to ask about the mold or her mom. Her father

was dead, and her mother's trail ended when she'd died decades ago.

This place underscored that she didn't know her mother—or this Florida version of her mother that had to have existed before Ali did.

All of that swirled around her head, and it threatened to stop her from sleeping at night or moving on with her own life during the day.

But The Sea Turtle Resort had other plans. And so did she. The morass of the past would not get in the way of this totally unexpected future she was trying to build.

There were actual tasks to be done, projects to be accomplished, and to-do lists to check off. Thanks to Faye and Blair, she had one year to make a go of this place as a viable business.

They all could have been millionaires if they sold it for what the real estate agent quoted. The Sea Turtle was two acres of gorgeous gulf front property that any developer would drool over, the sisters were told. They'd snatch it up and tear it down.

And that was the problem. Ali had grown to love the six cottages and funky inn next door. No one in their right mind would call this resort luxurious or Disney-level Florida living. But that was just what Ali liked. If she could turn it around, the goal was to make this little gem an affordable but magical spot for anyone who needed that ocean therapy like she did.

So, the to-do list called, and right now, that musty smell that was getting worse in the back bedroom of the Mango needed to be managed.

Ali fetched a ladder from the office cottage at the front of the property. She decided she needed to get her eyes on the roof of the cottage. And that meant the rickety old ladder.

The Sea Turtle Beach Cottage area was comprised of six cottages, each one a different bright color, situated around a little courtyard, but all pointed straight out to the gorgeous waters of the gulf. They were all angled to have a perfect ocean view. All were steps away from the surf.

She walked through the courtyard and realized the overgrown vegetation was an issue, but one she'd have to deal with on a different day. Ali envisioned weddings and parties in the courtyard in the coming years. But they would need to manicure the overgrown plants that she didn't know the names of. Faye would know. She'd know the names and be in love with each one. Ali wanted to hack away with a buzz saw, but Jorge said you weren't allowed.

Aack, stop, Ali Harris, you're getting ahead of yourself! First, deal with the funky-smelling Mango Mansion bedroom.

She propped the ladder on the side of the cottage. She pushed on it a few times.

It felt stable enough, and the cottage was only one story high. She'd be fine. Ali preferred wearing flip-flops, but for today's rugged work, she had switched out to overalls, a t-shirt, and work boots. If her father, Bruce Kelly, taught her one thing, it was the value of working with your hands. And you didn't wear the gorgeous vintage kaftans while snaking a drain or climbing a ladder. The vintage kaftans were courtesy of Didi. The woman had some fun and funky taste.

Ali carefully climbed each step of the ladder, holding her breath so that it would hold her. It did.

She surveyed the roof. The clay-tiled roof looked intact. There didn't appear to be loose or missing tiles. She decided to walk across the tiles to the area above the back bedroom of the Mango. It was a difficult balancing act, and she started to question how smart this was. Maybe she needed to call someone? Fortunately, it didn't take long to find something that did not look good.

The gutter where the roof met the exterior wall looked brown and not at all like it was draining water.

"Okay, well, that's gross," Ali said out loud. She needed a closer look and inched closer to the rotting bit of the roof. Would she need a whole new roof here? Could she get away with a repair in this area?

She looked around. There were palm fronds from the nearby trees draping all over this portion of the roof. She supposed it looked tropical and probably even helped keep the place shaded, but that didn't matter. Water was the culprit, and combined with salty ocean water, that was a recipe that was turning the Mango Mansion into the Moldy Mansion. That would not do if she were going to be a good host.

Ali took a few pictures, so she could consult with the internet on how best to deal with this hiccup. She carefully stood up and walked back to her ladder. She took each step down and, midway down, the ladder showed its age. The wooden step she was on snapped!

As she headed for the ground, Ali envisioned breaking a hip or cracking her head open. She didn't have time for either one!

But instead of landing with a thud, she landed on a stud. Well, a studly neighbor, at least.

"Whoa, you shouldn't be climbing on the roof without a spotter."

Henry Hawkins had Ali in his arms. Under his salt and pepper hair, he furrowed his brow at her. She scrambled to get her feet under her and reclaim an ounce of dignity.

"I'm not Didi and Jorge! I can use a ladder without a medic alert bracelet."

"I am not going to tell them you said that. They refuse to believe they're in their seventies, and you refuse to believe you're made of breakable parts. Beautifully made, I'll give you that, but breakable."

"You're a flirt and a nag. I'm not sure it's the best combination," Ali teased back, but she was lying. She liked everything about the man who owned the bar down the street and had become one of her closest friends in a matter of weeks. But friends, it must stay. She was still not quite divorced and about as unsure about romance as she was about cleaning a gutter on this Florida beach house. Did she like falling into his arms? Yes. Was it a good idea at this stage of her life? No.

"I know a roof guy, if you'd like me to call him. Not to nag." He gave her a dramatic wink just to let her know he was not about to stop flirting either.

"Yes, yes, I would. Now, how did I get so lucky to get saved from a broken hip? What's up?"

"I've also got a lead on how you might get more title information on this property."

Ali had discovered that her mother had owned the property and left it to the Kelly Sisters when she died in the 1980s. But she didn't have a clue about how her mother came to own it. The mystery was driving her more than just a little crazy. Her father was gone, and she knew almost nothing about her late mom's life. The property was an inheritance that her father had hidden from Ali, Faye, and Blair. And now that they had it, she just couldn't stop wondering about who her mother was, how she had this place, and why her father had never said a word about it!

He'd apologized to her on his deathbed, but she didn't know what he was sorry for, what he had done. Maybe it was just for keeping this a secret. But, regardless, learning her mother had owned this place and given it to them had opened a Pandora's Box of questions.

In her search for answers, Ali's search had hit dead end after dead end. County records prior to the mid-eighties were sketchy and relied on actual documents, many of which had been destroyed in a hurricane. If she had all the time in the world, maybe she could do more legwork, but she didn't have all the time in the world.

Ali had promised her sisters they wouldn't regret letting her try to keep The Sea Turtle. A quick sale could have led to a big windfall, but it would also lead to her husband getting half of the profit. Faye and Blair had made a sacrifice and agreed to let Ali make a go of The Sea Turtle as a business. She wanted this to be a viable income for all of them, but if, in a year's time, if it was still losing money, they'd sell.

Traipsing all over the state to find deed records from the eighties wouldn't help her get this place ready for tourist season. And that was the priority. But the minute Henry mentioned a lead, her ears perked up.

"Tallahassee, they've got some duplicates of county records. Moe said you can even request copies be sent. Stuff like that."

"Oh, well, that's something then. I mean, how in the world did my young mom own this place?"

Henry shrugged. "I thought you'd want to hear that, so you know, I came over, saved your backside, and have been abused for the effort."

She rolled her eyes. "How about I offer you some lemonade to show you how terribly sorry I am for calling you a nag?"

"I accept. I've got a half hour before I need to get back to The Seashell Shack for the rush."

"Perfect. Head out to the beach, and I'll join you in a second."

Henry saluted her like she was a general and grabbed two chairs for them to sit on to enjoy the view.

Ali had reveled in the hard work and challenge of getting The Sea Turtle in shape. Still, she also had learned from Didi, the property manager, and Erica, her new friend, along with Henry, that everything got better if you spent a little time looking at the ocean every day.

Gutters. Kids that ignored texts. And long-missing paperwork. All of that was tiny next to the immense and gorgeous ocean she now called her backyard.

Ali poured two glasses of icy cold lemonade and joined her not-boyfriend Henry on the Adirondack chairs.

Three

DIDI/BELINDA 1985

"Do you, Joetta Bennett, take Banks Armstrong to have and to hold from this day forward, in sickness and in health?"

Belinda watched her baby sister look at Banks Armstrong with love, actual love, in her eyes. Belinda loved Banks, too, as a friend. They'd grown up with Banks. He was practically a member of the family when they were kids, and now that they were all very grown it was about to be official. It was clear from the look on his face that Banks' dreams were coming true.

He'd loved Joetta since those old days growing up. The entire decade Joetta was gone, Banks would ask, "Hear anything from your sister these days?"

Belinda had lied. Joetta was traveling. Joetta was jet-setting. She was having the fabulous life that was her birthright.

Joetta was, in fact, living in Toledo, drinking the days away, and struggling as a wife and mother to three little girls.

Banks had no idea. Joetta regaled Banks about travels and a

fake life. Belinda backed her up. That's where Belinda learned how to lie. She'd learned to lie a lot thanks to Joetta.

But there was a huge problem with all of it. Joetta had three children: three little girls who thought their mother had died in a car wreck.

Belinda was not responsible for Joetta's choices. But they haunted her just the same. Belinda told herself that she was doing all she could to protect her little sister. The Gulfside Girls, as they used to be called, even concocted a plan to lure Bruce Kelly to Florida.

They'd signed The Sea Turtle over to the girls, in hopes it would convince Bruce to come here.

But he shut it all down.

Worse. He threatened to tell everyone in their high and mighty social circle that Joetta was a drunk, an unfit mother, and that she'd put her precious children's lives at risk when she got behind the wheel. Bruce Kelly was tough, and he played for keeps, Belinda discovered.

Still, part of her hoped that maybe Bruce would see, later, in time, that there was a little nest egg here. Maybe he'd see that Joetta was in AA now. Since she'd returned to Florida, the strongest thing she'd consumed was Shasta.

Joetta and Belinda had signed over the property, their inheritance from Grandfather. Belinda had taken care of all the legal paperwork and had tried to plead with Bruce. But he was done with the Bennett Sisters, and the Gulfside Girls were on their own with this.

Belinda had gone back to Joetta and told her to slow down and give it time. Don't make any rash decisions. Joetta was on a speeding train to get to the altar, again. Belinda wasn't wired the same, there was no need to get married just to be married. She wasn't sure she'd ever tie the knot. Joetta seemed to need to have a ring on her finger.

"I'm marrying Banks. I promised Bruce not to come back, and he signed the papers right away."

Joetta was focused. She was hard, even. Belinda wondered if Bruce Kelly's toughness was contagious. It had rubbed off on her once cotton candy sweet sister.

Belinda wanted to find a way to get the girls. She wanted to help soften Bruce and, short of that, get a lawyer, and get custody arranged.

"No, Bruce is right. I was a terrible mother. They're safer without me there."

Belinda hated hearing Joetta say that. But Joetta was clear eyed now that she had decided to marry Banks. The fight to keep her girls was gone. The fight to grab this alternative future, the future their parents had originally planned, was rapier sharp.

So, there they were, in the Polo Room of the country club. It was a small gathering. But all their parents were there, beaming. Well, maybe Banks' mother wasn't beaming, but she always looked sour, and the wedding of her son to the runaway youngest Bennett daughter was no exception.

Banks was joyful, and Belinda had to admit that Joetta was calm and beautiful in a new way. She'd blossomed since she'd been back. She thrived with Banks.

Blossomed.

As Belinda watched Joetta and Banks exchange vows, it hit her. Her eyes glanced down.

And she saw it. How had she missed it before?

Joetta had been under weight, scary skinny, when Belinda had scooped her up from Toledo and brought her back here.

And now there was a little fullness to her middle. The tiny Joetta had hints of curves.

Belinda tried not to let it show on her face, but anyone looking closely could see that Joetta was starting to show. Joetta was pregnant. Her baby sister was going to have another baby.

Banks and Joetta said their "I dos," and the gigantic ring Banks had insisted on circled Joetta's left ring finger.

Belinda's eyes darted from her sister's little bump to Bank's loving gaze to her parents to his parents.

"Speak now or forever hold your peace."

Belinda didn't say a word; she didn't even dare breathe.

"You may kiss the bride."

Joetta Bennett Kelly was now Joetta Armstrong. Only Belinda would know about the Kelly. Joetta Bennett Armstrong it was, now and forevermore.

Was this a second chance? Was this a last-ditch effort to find security?

Belinda didn't know what was going through Joetta's mind.

Bruce Kelly had threatened to take away any shred of a new life that Joetta had clawed from the sandy shores of Florida.

It was so easy to judge, but Joetta wasn't just protecting herself. She was protecting a baby. That was the one thing that redeemed her baby sister. Maybe this time, she'd get it right.

A tear escaped Belinda's eye. Everyone thought it was the wedding that made her cry. But it wasn't.

It was the secret she'd keep for her sister.

Bruce Kelly may be right. Maybe the girls were better off without the mess that came along with loving Joetta.

Four

FAYE

"Is that everything? For heaven's sake, if we have to turn around for a charger or something, I don't even know."

"It's good."

Sawyer and Faye were a team, it had been the two of them against the world for as long as she could remember.

She was prepared to yell, lay down ultimatums, propose alternative educational tracts, and threaten to withdraw financial support from Sawyer when she saw his latest round of grades at Ohio State University. She knew she had to do the tough love thing soon. But as a single mom, she was always the one to lay down the law. She did the grounding, she did the boundary setting, she did it all. And she'd have to kick his backside into gear about college.

And she was tired of it all. Did it ever end? The bad cop role?

Sawyer was smart enough to thrive in college, but he wasn't.

She had this idea that if she could get him through the first year, then he'd love it and hit his stride and get a degree and a job and be all grown up, and she could take a break. Maybe even hang it up as a single mom. She'd clock back in as a good cop Gigi or Kiki or whatever they called Grandmas these days.

But that wasn't happening. Sawyer wanted to drop out of college. She said no. But she could see that he was quiet quitting, she had heard that phrase on tv. It was a trend, quiet quitting. He was not saying, "I quit," instead he was just not going to class. He was ghosting OSU like it was his high school prom date.

The day after she decided to take a retirement buyout at the plant, she went to Columbus to be the strict mom. Her speech was set. He'd transfer to community college. He'd get grades up, and then he'd go to the University of Toledo like his cousins, and then and then and then.

But she opened her mouth, and what came out was a question she hadn't planned to ask.

"Do you want to go to the beach with me for a week or two? Help your aunt out while we figure out the next steps?"

Sawyer knew her, and he'd been prepared for stern mom, too. His relief at her offer was like a physical thing. His entire body unclenched.

"Are you sure you're Faye Kelly? I mean, did someone body snatch you?"

"I, uh, well, not that I know of. But here's the thing. I don't have the energy to get your life on track right now. I feel like mine is off track just as much. I need a little breather, and I feel like we both do."

"So, instead of lecturing me, you're going to take me to the beach?"

"Yep, heck, I'll even take you to Disney World if you take a shift or two driving down."

"Deal. And again, I am just checking. What's my middle name?"

"Conan, like the movie, not talk show."

"Yep, that's it, okay, so you're not body snatched. Let's hit the beach!"

Five

BLAIR

Blair Kelly was the baby.

Ali was their mother hen, and Faye was the classic middle child, driven to be seen by their father. Blair was the classic baby, and she knew it. Blair didn't have to struggle to get attention from Bruce, and he spoiled her. Doted on her in a way her sisters did not get. To her sisters' credit, they never seemed angry or jealous about it.

Blair never appreciated it quite enough when she was a kid or even a teen, but now she did appreciate it, more than ever. Unfortunately, that appreciation was too late.

Blair often wondered if that's why she didn't see the way Blake treated her as wrong at first. Because mostly he doted on her too, in the beginning. There she was in a strange town, alone, with no backup, and Blake swooped in. He lavished her with affection and the attention she missed by moving to the big city by herself.

She bonded with him, and she didn't see herself as tied to him.

Until one day, she was tied to him and somehow in an emotionally bad cycle. She knew it, but she couldn't seem to break it.

The latest issue? Blake saw Blair and the sale of The Sea Turtle for quick cash as his lottery ticket. And he wouldn't let it go.

Take this morning, for instance. She was checking her computer settings for an online work meeting and trying to get her hair figured out. *Was that another gray?* They were springing up like angry and wiry weeds in her auburn hair.

She looked at her image in the laptop camera and tried to smooth it down while Blake started literally spitting words at her. It was the same thing about a million dollars for the millionth time. She needed a glass of wine. Or several.

"The amount of money you are throwing away is repulsive." He was in jeans, no shoes, no shirt. It was a workday, and he wasn't at work. She used to think his six-pack abs were sexy. Now, she saw him more clearly. He was home, yelling at her, on a weekday, not working, just trying to work an angle.

Blair hadn't told Blake exactly how much money they were talking about in Florida.

It hadn't taken much for Faye to convince Blair to give Ali a year before selling The Sea Turtle. Blair was onboard; she could wait for millions if, in fact, the place really was worth millions. The chances of Ali being able to turn the place around were low. The odds were against her. But Blair owed her sisters this patience. The older she got the more she realized just how much she owed her older sisters. They were her surrogate mom, her buffer from the big bad world. The farther from them she got, the harder the world seemed to be.

Blake, however, didn't have that same well of gratitude or patience. He'd convinced himself that this was something he was entitled to. And that Blair agreeing to this "crazy plan" with her sisters was stupid. She was stupid, as usual.

"That money will be how we get the agency off the ground. The seed money alone turns us into multi-multimillionaires."

Us? If the property was worth what the real estate agent said it was worth, on paper at least, she was already a millionaire—well, a real estate one at least. Cash in hand, she had precious little. The conundrum had her thinking that maybe she needed something stronger than wine.

When she first met Blake, she thought he was the smartest person in any room. He was an account executive at an ad agency He told her he was on the way up. Shortly after that he'd missed out on a promotion. He'd explained to her that management at the agency were all idiots. He was outraged because they stole his ideas. He knew the agency would be doomed without him. So, he'd decided to go off on his own.

Blair believed in him wholeheartedly. She invested in Blake's start-up marketing firm with her savings.

That money was all gone now, and somehow, it was her fault.

She was supposed to manage the data and "do the computer stuff" he needed. "You handle the back end." That was, of course, on top of her actual full-time job. The one that she'd moved to Cincy for.

Blake had promised that it wouldn't be long, and she'd be able to quit her day job for the internet marketing company and be the VP of Blake's firm. It all sounded good. But just like Blake's muscular abs, his words were useless too.

Her day job was more important than ever, now. It was how they paid the rent.

When they first got together, it was her apartment, and he insisted he pay his fair share, 50-50, and now they were 100% supported by Blair. All the money she made disappeared into Blake's schemes.

Normally, that would give her confidence to know that she was contributing. She was the breadwinner. But the opposite was true. Blake seemed to resent her for doing better in her career than he did in his. Blake wasn't the smartest person in the room, he was just the loudest.

Looking at her computer screen, that morning, Blair had felt her hands shake, and she had a headache. It was stress. Blake was causing her to need that drink earlier in the day. And then two drinks, even earlier. She was managing the stress of it all, by taking the edge off.

Blair tried to nudge Blake back to his old job once it was clear he couldn't bring in a single client "out on his own."

She'd been nice about it. She was always trying to be nice.

"Like, if you just went back to marketing for one of the big firms, I know we'd be able to get out from under."

"Under? We're not under anything except your limiting ideas. I was listening to this podcast the other day and..."

He quoted a few bro dudes and then started making noises about starting a podcast of his own.

What? No. Goodness no.

His lack of attention on any one idea meant all his ideas were half-baked. Blake drained their accounts, one after another.

Blair knew what Blake would do with a windfall. She knew he'd want to get his hooks into it. So, she downplayed it. She showed him some of the jewelry and the dresses from her mom. Blair was able to sell them on eBay for a decent amount of cash. They were of amazing quality. Blair distracted Blake with these smaller windfalls and even used some of it to pay their rent. She didn't tell her sisters the details. Blair hated lying to them, but it was keeping the bills paid. One piece of her mother, then another. Blair didn't know her mother, but she knew they had expenses.

One day, he'd overheard Blair talking with her sisters about the property on Facetime. From that moment on, he wouldn't let it go.

He had it in his mind that there were tens of millions of dollars they could get. And that it should be theirs.

Lately, he'd been talking Faye and Ali down, saying he believed they were trying to keep it from them. He saw them as liars or cheats in some way. He'd never met them, but he knew they were taking advantage of her.

Blair knew better. She knew Ali had done everything she could to be a good mother to Blair and Faye. And she also knew it had been tough for Ali lately, thanks to Ted cheating on her. Ali was the one who took care of their father when he was sick. Ali deserved a chance at this dream coming true.

Blair put Blake off and downplayed what she knew. In her mind, she wondered how he saw fit to think it was his. They weren't even married. Blair had taken to heading to McGillivray's after work just to avoid Blake's schemes and questions. It was way easier there than being home.

Yet Blake kept circling back around to The Sea Turtle and pushing her to confront her sisters.

"Your sisters are stealing from you," Blake had said again that morning, "and that means they're stealing from me. You need to find out what an independent appraisal says about that property. I've got the name of a couple of great real estate agents that could turn this into a gold mine and then we can do what we really want."

"What do I really want?"

Blake had softened then; he'd pushed her too hard and realized it.

He'd wrapped her up in his arms and painted a picture of them working together, running a business together. They were a good team, he'd said.

"Don't worry, baby, I've got this. You just can't believe your sisters have your best interests at heart. You know I do. I'm your advocate, and they're not. Let me get you a glass, red or white?"

She hadn't argued; she was tired of arguing. But of course, later, prompted by her saying they needed to cut back on their cell phone bill, they'd had a massive argument.

That folded into Blake explaining how she wasn't good at business, and she was lucky Blake handled "all that."

Thinking back on the conflicts of the day, Blair reminded herself of her fierce and loyal sisters.

Blake was wrong, and they weren't trying to screw her over on the money. They were letting Ali pursue this dream, letting her spread her wings for once.

But Blake didn't buy it, and every day, there was a new little wormy thing he planted in her brain against her sisters.

She knew he was wrong, but also didn't know how to stop it. She was pushing forty, her bank accounts were on life support, and the man she once thought of as "the one" wasn't.

Blair felt trapped and didn't know how to describe it or get out of it.

She took the glass of red he poured her and drank it while he droned on and on and on.

Six

FAYE

Driving cross-country with her son was a new experience. He was almost twenty now, more man than boy, but still boy enough to expect her to book his doctor's appointments and produce his health insurance card. She'd provided a bubble for her son. This made her worry that he was prepared for exactly zero in life.

They'd decided to drive so Faye would have her car in Florida. She wasn't the best flyer, and having control of her own car when they got down to The Sea Turtle was very appealing. It was also a budget-friendly idea. She'd have her buyout, but she needed to be smart with cash since she was technically not working. Which was so weird to think about.

Plus, Ali might have errands they could help with, or she might decide she needed to explore, whatever the case may be. Faye and Sawyer had packed the car with her summer clothes, his video games, his skateboard, and weird bags of clay. Always with the clay. Before that, it was Play-Doh. That was her kid.

She laughed; she thought women were the ones with the reputation for overpacking, but her son had more bags and items than Eva Gabor moving into Green Acres.

Driving through Ohio was easy. They left Toledo, passed through Dayton, and would meet Blair for dinner on their way through Cincy. They may even sleep in Cincy but were playing it by ear.

It would be good to see Blair. She hadn't been in the same room with Blair since the funeral. And something seemed off about her little sister every time they Facetimed.

The met Blair in Cincinnati's Over the Rhine neighborhood, a historically German working-class area that, like a lot of similar places, had become a hip new hangout with gastropubs taking over old churches.

"Oh man, this place is cool. I think I could get a craft beer," Sawyer said.

"Sure, tell them you'd like it served in three years."

Sawyer wasn't twenty-one, but Faye knew that didn't stop him from having a beer or doing a keg stand at Ohio State.

"Ha, ha."

They pulled into the parking lot of Longfellow. Brick, ambiance, and beer were on the menu. Cincinnati had its charms, Faye admitted. She wished Blair didn't live so far away, but she could see the appeal.

Sawyer and Faye were seated and then kept an eye out for Blair. To Faye's surprise, her little sister arrived with a man she'd never seen. *This must be him, Blake*, Faye thought. The one too busy to come to their father's funeral, too busy to visit Toledo at the holidays, and so far, too busy to care about where Blair came from at all, in Faye's estimation.

Faye tried to get her attitude in check. In defense of Ali, she'd mouthed off to Ali's soon-to-be ex-husband Ted and, in the process, tipped Ted off to the notion that he should be receiving alimony. Not the other way around. Even though he was the cheating mid-life crisis, red car-driving bastard. Since she tended to defend her sisters aggressively, she had occasionally made things worse.

Faye put on a big smile to meet her sister's man. She couldn't even say "new man" since the two had been together for a while.

"I ordered us a plate of apps and soda pop. We're not drinking, but I hear getting a flight here is the thing to do."

Faye squeezed her sister in a tight hug, and Blair squeezed back. But there was something wrong, something amiss. Faye's Sister Spidey Sense was tingling.

Blair pulled back and looked at the waiter. "I'll have the hard cider please?"

"Yes, got it."

Only after her order did Blair turn to Sawyer. She messed up his floppy blond hair, and all was well. They all arranged themselves around the circular table.

"So, impromptu visit to Florida? You're usually more of a planner—I mean, not Ali levels—but this was out of the blue, yeah?"

"Yeah, well, I didn't want to tell you over the phone, but I'm retired."

"What!"

"Yeah, she's got a Golden Buckeye Card, a walker, the works."

Faye hit Sawyer on the arm. "I can still take you down," Faye said.

"Oh, right, none of us but Bruce have been able to take this one down since he was fifteen," Blair pointed out. Sawyer was tall, strong, and now filling out. The lanky teenage years were being replaced with something new, more mature.

Time is flying, Faye thought, not for the first time.

Sawyer was twice the size of his beloved aunts and had been for years.

Blake didn't join in the family ribbing. In fact, his body

language was stiff and edgy, like he truly did have somewhere else to be. Like he was too busy even to have a meal with his girlfriend's family.

He shifted in his chair and then cleared his throat.

Blair swallowed and looked from her boyfriend back to Faye. The waiter brought out the drinks. Blair immediately grabbed the hard cider and took a long pull. Her sister had the look of someone who'd had a very tough day. She then turned to her nephew with a request.

"Sawyer, would you do me a favor? I wonder if you'd go out to the gift shop area and pick out a sweatshirt for Aunt Ali. I want to send it along with you guys since I can't come down." Sawyer knew when he was being shooed out, and he looked to Faye to be sure that was okay. She was the boss of him, still.

"Get one for yourself too," Faye said, giving Sawyer her credit card.

A look passed between Blake and Blair as though something had happened that they expected. Something wrong.

What did I do?

With Sawyer out of earshot, Blair timidly began. "I want to ask you about the Florida property. I think we might have been too hasty."

"Hasty?"

"Well, in giving this year timetable. I think we might, uh, reconsider, or maybe..." Blair looked down at the cocktail napkin and not into Faye's eyes. Then, as soon as Sawyer was out of sight, Blair looked at Blake as though asking him permission for something.

Faye did not understand the source of their conflict or discomfort—clearly, something was wrong between the two of them. Was this always the way, or was this something new? Faye felt a sharp pang of guilt in her chest as she realized she should've made a better effort to understand what was happening in her sister's life.

Blair spoke up again. "I was wondering if we could talk about this whole arrangement."

"Arrangement?" Faye asked.

"Well, this whole year situation," Blair repeated. She grabbed her hard cider and took another generous gulp.

Is this a liquid courage sort of thing?

Then Faye realized what Blair was talking about: The Sea Turtle and the one year they'd given Ali to make a go of it. She thought the arrangement might be too restrictive—one year really wasn't enough—so she was happy, even relieved, to think that Blair felt the same.

"I'm so glad you mentioned this," Faye said. "I feel like one year isn't enough. We really need to give Ali a chance to make this work."

Blair looked like she might cry.

What is going on? Faye wondered.

"Well, no, it's more like...I'm concerned," Blair sputtered. She was searching for words. She wasn't the confident, fun, sweetly spoiled baby of the family. Something was off, and Faye had no doubt the blame was Blake's.

She'd just met the guy, but everything about him was giving her bad vibes—the way he walked a little bit on his toes, the way his beard was groomed to perfection. No man should be that well-groomed. His name, his whole obnoxious outfit—everything gave her bad vibes. The worst part, though, was how her sister somehow seemed diminished alongside this man. And how she held on to her glass like it was about to run away.

And then Blake finally opened his mouth. "This is a ridiculous financial proposition. You are losing millions of dollars by not selling immediately."

Zero to mansplain in three seconds. That had to be some sort of record.

And it was a familiar tune. Ali's husband had the same thoughts. At least Ted had put in decades of husband work before acting like an ass, though. But this guy? He wasn't even married to Blair. Faye was pretty sure she could shut this down, but she shouldn't have to.

Shouldn't it be Blair saying something, sticking up for Ali, sticking up for their decision?

As if on cue, Blair tried to interject, "Well, it's just that we could—"

But Blake interrupted her, jabbing the table with his finger. It seemed to Faye as if he would've put his hand over Blair's mouth if he could.

"It is clear you ladies don't understand finance or real estate or even the hospitality industry in Florida," Blake said. "Timing is everything. A hurricane could hit. The market value could plummet right now. It's a choice spot on the beach. But the clock is ticking in a way you do not comprehend, as I've explained to Blair."

Faye wanted to talk to Blair, but Blake kept interjecting, so she turned her gaze to him. The Kelly Sisters really did not know how to pick men. That was a therapist session for another day, though. Right now, it was time to make things very clear with this blowhard. It was time to Kellysplain right back.

"Blake, I just met you. I don't know what your background is, but this is really between my sister and me. It doesn't have anything to do with you."

The muscle in the back of Blake's jaw pulsed. Faye's eyes dropped to the table as Blake covered Blair's fine-boned hand with his much larger one. Faye didn't miss the fact that Blair winced. Who was this stranger telling her how to handle her sister and trying to change a decision that had nothing to do with him? She wanted to laugh—it was preposterous—but Blair wasn't in a joking mood. What Blair looked like was defeated or even scared. Blair's awkward body language conveyed more than her words with this man policing the conversation.

Faye reined in her natural propensity to mouth off. It had

turned out badly with Ted. She didn't want to make things worse for Blair.

She struggled to find a compromise, something that would satisfy Blake and get her the heck out of this weird dynamic. She pretended she was on the plant floor in the middle of a heated argument between the safety inspector and Dusty Sporling. Her job was to get them to cooperate and stay on task. She'd use that voice now.

"How about this? We're heading down to Florida. I'll get boots on the ground. I'll help Ali for a couple of weeks. Sawyer can, too. I'm sure Ali has this all under control, and I know you see it as a bad financial decision, but I think it's going to be a life-changing good decision long-term. It's the long game here, Blake."

"For you and Ali, that seems obvious," Blake said.

What was he implying? That we're trying to cheat Blair?

She wanted scoff, but instead, she tried to smile, to reassure Blair.

Blair nodded along with Faye.

In agreement, see? We're in line together, sisters. Got it, buddy?

But Blake was not pacified.

Faye wondered why she was trying to pacify this man—because that was what she was doing, dealing with him as though he was owed something.

"I have the name of an appraiser. I'm going to give you that name, and you need to get them on the property to get the real numbers and the real information. Otherwise..." Blake started.

"Otherwise, nothing," Blair interjected. She smiled brightly, and her voice was unnaturally high and cheerful. "A good appraisal is good for everyone, right?"

"Sure," Faye said, though they did have a decent appraisal already.

Blair looked like a caged animal. Faye felt like she should stay in Cincinnati, like she needed to do something to snap her sister out of whatever was happening here.

Just then, Sawyer returned with two long-sleeve T-shirts.

"These are cool, right?" he asked.

The conversation abruptly stopped. Thank goodness. She didn't want Sawyer to see how distressed his aunt was. This was between the sisters, and that's how it should stay. Blair seemed under Blake's control in some way.

Faye recognized this dynamic. She'd lived this dynamic. She'd understood what that was like—she'd been in that situation with her husband, Sawyer's dad. If Blake were that flavor of man, he'd blame Blair for anything Faye said or did. Faye wasn't about to cause trouble for her baby sister.

So, she backed down. She agreed. She de-escalated—for once, for Blair. She included Blake in the conversation as though he deserved it. Because she knew how things could get worse if he perceived them trying to go around him.

"Blair, I understand your concerns, and they're good concerns. The last thing we want is to do something rash or financially stupid. Send me that name, and I'll make sure to call. Does that sound OK to everybody?"

Blair didn't answer. She looked to Blake for his opinion. This was bad.

I need to let Ali know what's going down here, Faye thought. *And I need to talk to Blair without Blake sitting there.*

"Alright, I'll send you the information but let me make something perfectly clear. I am here to protect Blair. You two sisters think you're going to pull something over on her because she lives here, she's not savvy, she's the youngest. But you've got another thing coming."

Not savvy? Her sister was brilliant in Faye's eyes.

It felt like a slap in the face. Faye wanted to slap back, but instead, she stood up.

"I think Sawyer and I need to get back on the road. It's a long drive. It's good to see you," she said, holding out her hand. She squeezed Blair's hand, and Blair squeezed back.

"Come on, kiddo, onward to Atlanta. I-75, ya know, Cincy and Atlanta traffic are the worst!" Faye was blathering on now; she needed to get away from this man and figure out why her sister didn't do the same.

Faye was livid. She was also afraid—afraid for her baby sister in a way she hadn't realized she needed to be.

Seven

ALI

Ali's mind swirled with questions as she continued to get the Mango and Strawberry cottages ready for guests. She believed the answers could make or break the business she was trying to launch.

What were the elements of hospitality that made a great day? Why do people love a place? What did a world-class luxury hotel offer that she could do better? What was totally out of reach for this business?

Those were the questions that kept her up at night.

She would have two families here for spring break. Sure, she'd like to be fully booked, but she wasn't ready for that just yet. Ali's first experience with guests included shouting and disgust over the state of the swimming pool. Just a few weeks ago it was a swampy mess. When she first got to The Sea Turtle Didi and Jorge couldn't keep up. The pool wasn't the only thing in disrepair, plus, the phone was out of service, and they didn't have a website for online bookings. Overcoming all that with two bookings felt like a victory. It wasn't the ultimate goal, but it was better than where she'd started with The Sea Turtle.

She had a lot of things to do to market the place beyond word of mouth, but for now, she had to focus on smaller scale successes. Ali would make The Sea Turtle great and then figuring out how to spread the word would come next.

Ali focused on creating an experience for those two families she had booked.

Most places in Florida these days were large operations—hospitality giants. She wasn't that, by a long shot. But she also knew how to host. After years of running the largest convention and event space in Toledo, Frogtown Convention Center, she knew how to take care of details. She prided herself on the fact that vendors and guests felt like royalty at Frogtown.

The Sea Turtle was nowhere near the size of her old venue. There were fewer customers. Each one would be the king of the place. That was her goal. Her challenge.

Ali wanted each funky little beachfront cottage to be a little oasis. When you walked into the Mango, it smelled like ocean breezes, salty air, and just a hint of cocoa butter. She'd put in a new floor—that was her biggest expense. She'd learned how to install a toilet by herself, which was not her favorite task. *Ew, wax ring.*

She'd taken down the old draperies and linens and replaced everything with light, airy fabrics. Ali needed more personal touches in the space because she was aiming for an old Florida style —just enough to remind guests that they weren't at home but on vacation.

The main room of the Mango had a sitting area and kitchenette. It wasn't huge, but just big enough for a family of four or five to play Scrabble or cards.

Ali had wiped down all the kitchenette cabinets and decided they didn't need to be repainted; they just needed a good scrub. She replaced the old dishes with colorful melamine ones she'd found at Goodwill. They were indestructible and fun, adding a touch of lightness to the kitchen. Most of what she found was thrifted. It reminded her of her mother, thrifting. She had distant memories of walking down the tree-lined sidewalks of Kenwood all the way to Manchester, where Old Orchard, her neighborhood, turned into Ottawa Hills, the fancy neighborhood. Her mom said Ottawa Hills had "the good stuff."

Her mother was so good at negotiating, eyeing things, and inspecting them for damage. It was a long-ago memory, but Ali believed that every time she found a Goodwill or a Garage Sale with "the good stuff," her mother had led her there. Our Lady of Perpetual Thrift wasn't an actual saint, of course, but it was who she prayed to.

Haven Beach had a few good places, but slowly Ali found neighborhoods outside Haven Beach with tag sales and estate sales. When she couldn't thrift it, Target was the next best thing! Target didn't exist when she was a kid. Her mom would have loved Target. One year, when Target teamed up with Lily Pulitzer, Ali figured her mom must have directed that merger from the great beyond!

Between repairs and shopping excursions, she made sure that whatever a family might need would be inside The Mango. She found a blender, a toaster, and a mini microwave so they wouldn't have to leave if they didn't want to.

The refrigerator, though—well, that was a different story. It was disgusting and had to go. She replaced it with a small but fully functional retro-style appliance, which looked adorable. Since it was called the Mango, she decided to go all in on the theme. She got little mango soaps, a mango art print from HomeGoods, and a mango bathmat.

The Mango, just like all the cottages, had two bedrooms. One bedroom was originally furnished with two twin beds. For the Mango, though, Ali decided to go one step further and put in bunk beds so as many kids as possible could stay there.

She remembered a long-ago trip to Disney when the kids were

little. They didn't stay in a Disney hotel but rather a Holiday Inn. It had a double bed and a set of bunks, zero luxury on any scale. Except the bunks had curtains you could close, and the kids pretended they were camping. They talked about that place for years after.

Remembering that, Ali put little J-hooks on the ceiling of the top two bunks to recreate the camping effect. Her littlest guests could imagine they were camping, even though they were inside. It was the same concept as buying an expensive toy that wound up in the junk heap while the kids made believe with the big cardboard box.

Ali put effort into making the primary suite a little more grown up.

Maybe honeymooners would stay here, but it was more likely to be families. She fit the biggest bed she could in there. It was originally a double, but now it was a queen. You'd have to cuddle up a bit, but it was comfortable. She found adorable sheets and linens and a cozy seat for the corner.

Since she knew families sometimes needed space to work, even on vacation, she found a little desk and chair. If Dad needed to log in or Mom had a Zoom call, they could still do it here. In the small closet, she made sure there were extra towels, extra sheets, and even extra beach towels. There was nothing you would need in the bathroom that she hadn't stocked: sunscreen, shampoo, conditioner, and even a blow dryer. The worst thing in the world was to forget a blow dryer while traveling. But no one who came to The Sea Turtle would have to worry about that.

She felt proud of how it had come together. This was an affordable, dare she even say, stylish place to enjoy the beach. The Mango wasn't new or even very big, but little by little it was becoming luxurious in its quirky way. She just had to do that five more times for the rest of the cottages.

Still, one last look at the Mango made Ali feel hopeful that she could pull this off—create an experience for her guests at The Sea

Turtle. It was one of six cottages, and she had given zero effort toward the inn next door but so be it. One room at a time was her mantra.

The next bit, though, was going to take some help from her friends, which she now had. Her new bestie was Erica, and she owned the café up the road.

Erica would be key in making sure every guest at The Sea Turtle had a free breakfast if they wanted it. Ali had arranged with Erica to have coffee delivered to the main office every day, along with two trays of pastries. If you didn't want to cook or didn't get to the grocery store, you could always pop into the office for a doughnut and some of the best coffee in Mangrove County.

Ali had done all of this by working from sunup to sundown, almost every moment since her sisters had agreed to let her take this on.

Every night, she fell into bed, nervous about whether she was doing the right thing but also exhausted from the hard work. She had accomplished a lot in a short time, but the next step would require more than just her efforts—it would take a village.

Eight

FAYE

They had reached critical mass. Cracker Barrel was an hour and a half behind them. Faye's coffee and Sawyer's giant glass of juice were making their presence known.

It was time to find a rest stop!

Faye scanned each exit's billboards for a suitable place to pull off the highway.

From the moment Faye knew she was pregnant, she was in the driver's seat, just like now. Bud wasn't ready to be a dad. He'd made that clear a million times. But she was a mom to her boy before she even knew he was a boy.

Buddy liked to boss her around, but that wasn't the same as actually being the boss or, more specifically, being the adult.

From the second the blue line appeared on the pregnancy test, Faye was the mom, the adult, and, in this case, the driver. She'd get her baby boy where they needed to go. Faye was both mother and father to Sawyer. She took care of the cars, the bills, the house, the permission slips, and, most importantly, Sawyer.

Taking care of herself? Self-care? That made her laugh to think about. Who had time for self-care? She plucked stuff, died her roots, and used lip gloss. That was all she had time for.

These thoughts and millions of others rolled around her head as they rolled south from Toledo to Cincinnati to Kentucky and now to Tennessee.

And very quickly, all thoughts were being pushed away by one thought. They both needed to find a rest stop fast. But the same mission guided her actions. Be a good mom, be a good dad, provide the best she could for her son. And right now, that meant a decent place to, well, go.

There weren't family restrooms back in her early days as a mom. She used to have to bring him into the ladies' room and later, when he got bigger, stand guard outside the men's. That got her some strange looks now and then.

She remembered being so tired some days when Sawyer was little. She was always so stressed, so always "on."

Now that Sawyer was almost grown—well, physically anyway —some of that was easier. Except, of course, now he was screwing up at college, and he appeared to have zero direction in life.

Was that his dad in him? Ugh, shake it off, Faye, and find a bathroom!

The first exit didn't look so good; it was just a gas station. But Faye didn't stand on ceremony—if there were a gas station, it would be fine. Unfortunately, when they got to the bathroom, there was an "Out of Order" sign on the door.

"Man," Sawyer said, looking around, possibly considering a nearby field.

Faye lifted an eyebrow at her son. "I didn't raise an animal. Come on, we can make it to the next exit."

The next exit, unfortunately, was 10 miles away. They finally pulled into a town they'd never heard of, somewhere in the middle of Tennessee. They took a right turn off the exit and kept following signs that read, "Rest Stop – 2 Miles."

"Two miles?" Sawyer questioned.

But she was committed. They'd taken a sidewinding way for a decent bathroom, and by golly, she'd find one!

"Look, I've gotta go, you've gotta go. If we don't find it in another two miles, I'll let you go in the field. Heck, *I'll* go in the field."

This time, it was Sawyer's turn to raise an eyebrow.

"Mom, please don't make me want to throw up."

Faye answered with a shrug. But eventually, they found it.

Knobby's Corner, read the sign over the log cabin-style building.

Knobby's was nestled in a wooded area, with no Walmart or McDonald's anywhere in sight. It had a gas pump and an outbuilding that housed a couple of restrooms that appeared to be open and in working order. Faye was ready to send a thank you prayer up for that.

Sometimes, blessings came in surprising ways.

She parked her vintage Wrangler, and they headed toward the restrooms. Sawyer peeled off to his, and Faye went to hers. She took care of things, checked her hair in the mirror, and washed her hands. There was no one else in the restroom, so she walked outside, looked around, and waited for Sawyer.

She happened to notice a beat-up pickup truck with a guy leaning on the truck's bed. He was looking her up and down. *Move along, buddy*, she thought. But instead of ignoring him, she returned his gaze with her most severe resting bitch face. It didn't seem to have much of an effect, so Faye looked around some more. Not seeing Sawyer, she decided to head inside the convenience store. *Creeps are everywhere*, she though, even at Knobby's hole-in-the-wall, middle-of-nowhere corner store.

Inside, things only got stranger. A skinny guy was behind the cash register with a piece of beef jerky hanging from his mouth like it was a cigarette. Faye realized she probably needed to buy something. She felt a little bad that, despite using the restroom, she hadn't planned on it. But she was here now, right?

She glanced around. A magazine rack revealed yet another reason to trust her darker instincts: *Big Jugs Magazine*, *Sharp Blade Weekly*, and something about Woodland Creatures. This was not a great place to be shopping for snacks. That might be squirrel jerky hanging from the skinny cashier's mouth.

As Faye wandered around, trying to find something else to buy, the door to the store opened, and in burst Sawyer. He scanned the room, locked eyes with his mother, and made a beeline for her.

"Let's go," he said.

"What? I was going to buy something..."

Sawyer shook his head, "We need to get out of here *now*." He grabbed Faye's arm and guided her toward the door.

She was taken aback. When had he become the one to take charge? She tried to calm him down. "It's fine, Sawyer."

But he wasn't listening. "Let's go, Mom," he repeated.

They reached the door, and Sawyer opened it. He looked both ways, as if they were in a spy movie, before hustling her toward the Jeep. He opened her door first, then walked around to the passenger side.

Faye gave him a questioning look. "What the heck is going on?"

Sawyer pointed behind them to the man she'd seen at the pickup truck; he now had a sidekick, and they were headed toward her Jeep. They didn't look friendly, or maybe they looked too friendly. Either way, the vibe was bad. Very bad. The rearview mirror showed them moving in.

"I heard those two talking about you while I was in the stall," Sawyer said under his breath. "They're not good guys. Let's just say that."

Faye's heart sank. As she put the Jeep in reverse, the two men planted themselves behind her vehicle.

She slammed on the brakes.

"What the heck?" she muttered.

Sawyer kept his eyes on the guys. "I told you. They watched you go into the restroom. They didn't know I was with you."

Faye put the car in drive and did a quick three-point turn to avoid hitting the two men. She pulled out of the rinky-dink rest stop with her tires squealing on the pavement. She kept looking in the rearview as they headed back toward the on-ramp for I-75.

"Wow, that was something," she said, her voice shaky.

"Yeah, I almost flipped out when I realized they were talking about you," Sawyer admitted.

"Well, your mom isn't chopped liver," Faye replied, her face a little red at the thought of what Sawyer had just implied.

"They weren't exactly *Golden Bachelor* material, Mom."

"I appreciate you looking out for me, son," she added, her voice softening.

They merged onto I-75 and left the small, strange rest stop behind.

As they drove, Faye felt a little lighter, though the situation had been odd. For the first time, she realized that Sawyer wasn't always her responsibility. He could be an adult in a pinch. Her baby boy was becoming a man.

Sawyer was someone who could not only take care of himself but also a man who cared about his mom and looked out for her instead of the other way around, like it had been for so long.

She smiled as the miles piled up between them, and Knobby's Corner and Tennessee turned to Georgia.

Onward to Florida!

Nine

BLAIR

Blake was still angry. He was able to get Blair to do what he wanted. But Faye? No way. Her boyfriend had come up against the toughest Kelly Sister when he tried to boss Faye around.

The lunch had degenerated so fast. On the way home in the car, Blake berated Faye and her.

"She's an idiot. You're letting a fired autoworker run a million-dollar investment."

"She wasn't fired; she was offered a buyout. That happens."

"Fired."

Blair wanted to correct him again, but it would be wasted words. He was never wrong.

She would let him cool down. The best way to do that was to agree quietly. When they got back to their place, she looked at the clock. It was four. That was practically evening.

Blair got out a bottle of wine and poured herself a glass. She'd fall asleep early, or she hoped so.

She opened her phone and was scrolling when Blake came into

the sitting room. He threw a box on the coffee table in front of her. It startled her, and she jumped out of her skin.

"What are you doing with that?"

The box was from their mother! She was slowly selling some but also keeping pieces too. Blake had nothing to do with any of it and it made her angry that he was even touching it, much less throwing it around.

Blake had a string of pearls in his hand. "I'm taking this."

"What?"

"It's worth twelve hundred dollars. I saw your internet search."

"That's an heirloom from my mom." Blair watched as Blake shook the beads in the air.

"You didn't even know your mom, and we need the cash. Consider this a downpayment."

"On what?"

"I need to put a deposit on the office space and here we have it. When you sell that property, you can head to the pawn store and get them back."

"But they could sell them, and I'd never see them again. Let's find the cash a different way."

"Your ability to understand business is zero. And old lady jewelry sitting in a box is doing nothing to help us get ahead. So, like I said, I'm taking this and putting it to good use."

Blair stood up.

"Those are mine. Those are my sisters'."

"What's yours is mine. We're practically married, remember." He winked at her, and it made her skin crawl.

Was it that moment? Maybe it was. Something inside changed. He'd acted terribly when he met her sister and nephew. And now he was stealing her mom's pearls.

She'd taken a fair amount of crap from Blake because she loved him. Well, used to love him. He was a terrible person, and she needed to get out of this relationship.

Blake had never hurt her physically. His abuse was all emotional. She watched him leave with her mother's pearls.

Later, Blair packed a suitcase. But she wasn't quite ready. She'd need cash and a new crate for Darla, her beloved cat.

Soon, very soon, she'd leave Blake for good.

Blair hid her suitcase in the back of the closet. She made a mental list of what she needed to do to make a clean break.

And then she found her wine glass. She drained it, so she poured herself another.

Ten

DIDI

Didi put on her most "little old lady" face, voice, and body language in hopes of getting exactly what she needed. She approached the counter and pretended to be completely confused and helpless. Well, that was one good thing about looking old; people believed that act, and it might get you a door opened, or a heavy grocery bag loaded into the car.

Or completely ignored.

It appeared the young man at the counter had been raised right. He wanted to help the little old lady.

"What are you after, ma'am?"

Didi retrieved a piece of paper from her pocketbook and read it in the same way she read the Christmas Lists she received from her grandchildren to the nice kids in blue shirts at Best Buy.

This was still part of her act, though. She knew exactly what she needed.

"I need the original document of title for the property, 13 Gulfside, on Haven Beach, please," she recited, smiling.

The man in the khaki Dockers and short-sleeved dress shirt typed something into the computer.

Why in the world did they still make short-sleeved dress shirts? Alas, years of working at the country club had given her an aversion to business casual dressing.

"Okay, I think we've got the right box indexed. Let me go get that."

"Thank you."

The young man at the counter walked down the aisle and opened a drawer in a tall file cabinet. He rifled through and mumbled something as he did it. Finally, he grabbed a manilla folder, slid it out, and returned to the counter to show her.

"What year do you think it would be?"

"1980-something, I think."

"Oh, gosh, okay. That's going to be even farther back. Those aren't all digitized yet. This is only to 1995."

This time, Didi decided to follow the young man. She scooted around the counter, and the two of them walked a little farther down row of cabinets.

Didi kept a smile on her face. She did not want this young man to know anything was amiss. Or that she had subterfuge on her mind.

"Alright, so you said...what was the address again?"

"13 Gulfside."

"Okay, this file drawer here." He pulled out the file drawer and started fingering through each of the file folders. "Here it is."

An office phone rang, and then the door opened to the lobby. There was another citizen with a question. What luck.

The man handed the file to her.

"You can take a look at it over there if you'd like. I've got to answer that phone and deal with—"

"—Oh, you've been so helpful. Go, go!" She smiled again. She didn't want him paying any more attention to her.

She took the folder, walked over to a table, and opened it up. There it was: the deed to The Sea Turtle Resort and Cottages.

She went back as far as she could. There they were—the original owners.

Her grandparents. They'd given it directly to Belinda and Joetta, the original Gulfside Girls. They'd skipped her father and mother. Her mother scorned the address, the accommodations, and really the beach itself. Her father had a soft spot for it, though. Maybe that's why her mother didn't want it. She also remembered hearing that it was the bad side of the beach. And that none of their mother's friends were that far south on Gulf.

Her mother and father got millions from her grandparents. This little property was barely a blip. But Belinda knew it was a gem—the real family jewels.

This would be the exact trail that Ali was looking for—a trail that would eventually lead right to her and the secret Didi had kept for decades.

Didi looked around. *Are there security cameras around here?*

The young man who had helped her was now knee-deep in a phone conversation and had two people waiting at the counter.

She didn't see any cameras. But it didn't hurt to be extra cautious.

She pretended to drop the file on the floor. *Oopsy!*

As she picked the contents up, she slyly slid the old document into her giant purse, leaving the outer folder on the table.

It was closed, and nothing in it went farther back than what Ali already knew. The deed to the place started in the 1980s from Joetta to the girls. There is no record of Didi signing it to Joetta or her grandparents as the original owners.

Didi took the slightly skinnier file and returned it to the cabinet, but this time, she put the file in the wrong drawer.

Just a little more insurance against Ali's inquiries. It was an innocent mistake, filing it one drawer down.

Joetta wouldn't have appreciated how much Didi had done for

the lie. How much Didi had protected her baby sister. She felt she'd failed her nieces. But now it was right. Well, almost right.

Hopefully, this brought Didi more time with Ali, Faye, and God willing, Blair; she so wanted to meet Baby Blair.

Didi quickly looked around, reset her best "old lady" face, and walked back toward the reception area.

"Thank you so much," she said to the young man, who was now busy helping a builder with some sort of lot-line question.

Jorge was waiting in the truck, and he was not happy.

"Do you really think this is necessary? You're acting like you're in a heist movie."

"I just got my nieces back in my life. If they found out what we did, there's no telling how they'd react."

"They're going to find out, and you should be the one to tell them."

"I can't do that. I can't betray my sister, and I can't break their hearts again."

"Didi."

He was scolding her again. She brushed it off. If you couldn't brush off the disapproval of your long-time husband, what kind of wife were you anyway? He was not her boss. In this case, he was just the getaway car.

"Jorge, now come on. We've got to get back on the road. Ali is expecting us. It's going to be a big month for her—her first official spring break with new guests. There's a million things to do."

Jorge replied, "Yeah, that is true. Silvio is going to meet me at the pool. Ali shouldn't have that on her plate, along with the rest of it. That pool is going to take at least a couple of days to go from green to clear. I also think the tiles aren't all there or intact."

"See, it's all fine. Don't you worry about this little caper."

"I am worried about you."

Jorge loved her, and she loved him. She loved that his life did not include a big secret or family intrigue, except for the flavor of intrigue she'd dragged him into.

"I'll figure it out. This just gives me time to do just that!"

She and Jorge held hands for a moment, but they let go once they merged onto the highway; it was always ten and two on the wheel at their age.

As they headed back to Haven Beach, Didi was focused on helping Ali make a go of it. And getting Faye settled there, too. What if Faye stayed? It would be a dream come true!

A dream deferred and one that had emerged from a nightmare beginning.

Was it too much to hope for?

Or was it something they all deserved after so long a wait?

Didi patted the outside of her purse. She had the proof Ali was looking for, and she'd share it when the time was right.

But that time wasn't right now.

Eleven

ALI

Ali selected the Strawberry Hideaway for her second renovation project. It was also directly on the beach. She'd stayed there and knew what needed to be done.

She looked at the checklist that she had written. She was feeling a little bit unsure but still confident that she could pull this off. She knew two families would be arriving on Good Friday.

The Dean family was scheduled to show up around lunchtime. The Dean family consisted of mom, Sheri; dad, Will; and two sons, Will Jr. and little Lou. A family of four—she could handle a family of four. They would be staying in the Strawberry.

The larger group, the Bowmans, would be in the Mango. She had a soft spot for the Mango and hoped they would, too. The Bowman family consisted of mom, Carrie; Aunt Betty; dad, Kevin; and three kids. It would be tight, but she was confident she could make sure they had a lovely stay.

Today, though, it was all about Faye and Sawyer. She'd gotten a text earlier in the morning that they were crossing the border from

Georgia into Florida. She'd hoped they'd be there before sunset. Sure enough, when they pulled in, it was a sight for sore eyes.

She missed her family.

She'd felt a nearly instant connection to Didi, Jorge, and even Henry and Erica, but her people were in Toledo, more or less. Faye couldn't wait to have them here.

When Faye got out of the Jeep, Ali felt something critical realign in her. Ali and Faye were bonded for life, and that bond could easily withstand distance, but it was way better to be close.

Ali ran up to her little sister and wrapped her in a huge hug. She knew her sister was stressed out, overwrought over how her company had discarded her. Ali knew what it was like to be under-valued. Faye was going to feel shell-shocked, but hopefully, some beach time would help. It helped her, sometimes, like magic.

Ali took in all that was her nephew, Sawyer, next. He'd filled out in the best way. Gone was the "go team" look. He almost looked, as she'd say, like a man—a cute man. Though with shaggy blonde hair, he looked as though he was born to be on the beach instead of in Toledo, Ohio.

"Aunt Ali, you've got a savage tan," Sawyer said.

She wore sunscreen all the time, but she had to admit that a little color on her legs made her happy, too. She vowed always to cover her face and her chest, but darn it, her legs needed a little something something!

"You guys haven't checked into a hotel yet, have you?" Ali asked.

"No, we haven't. But we've got a reservation at the Court-yard," Faye said.

"Then you've got time. check-in is all day over there. I've got some food for us. I just want you guys to enjoy being in Florida the next couple weeks."

"Enjoy? No, we're going to be working," Faye replied.

Ali looked at Faye. Work, work, work. She understood that. But Didi had directed her to just breathe when she first got here.

Now, she was going to try to do the same for her little sister. Tell her just to breathe, take in the salt air for a day or two, and things won't look quite as bad. Well, that was what Ali hoped, anyway.

After hugs and kisses and checking up on the weather in Toledo, the three of them went out to the beach. Ali had prepared a Grand Finale charcuterie, and before long, Didi and Jorge showed up to fuss over Faye.

When Jorge saw Sawyer, his eyes lit up.

"Oh, this is exactly what we need," Jorge said.

Ali was not sure what he was talking about, but it wouldn't hurt Sawyer to spend some time with Jorge. Jorge could fix just about anything, and now that his hip was a little bit better, he was getting around better. In fact, Ali was thinking maybe it wasn't time for the two of them to retire yet. Maybe they had a little bit of life in them before she would be totally solo at The Sea Turtle.

Jorge took Sawyer to the swimming pool.

*Ah-h*a, Ali thought. *Maybe that's what he's up to.*

Ali turned to Faye. "You know, he doesn't have to work when he's here."

"Oh, don't worry," Faye said. "If there's a reason to get out of work, he'll figure it out."

"Oh, don't be too harsh. There were a lot of decisions that he had to make during his freshman year. It can be overwhelming." She remembered her two kids, only a few years out from their first years of college. "So, what's he thinking?"

"He's thinking that he can become a professional pottery wheel spinner or something like that. Who knows? I need him to get a good job with health benefits. It's real hard to convince a nineteen-year-old they need health benefits."

"Well, he didn't up to a few days ago, right?"

"Right."

"So, how's the package they gave you?"

"It's okay. I mean, I will have health insurance, which is good and with my retirement pension, I'm okay on that score. But not set for life, you know? And Sawyer can stay on my plan until he's 26. Thanks, Obama."

They laughed, but it was no joke. Keeping your kids in health insurance was an important reason to stay working. Ali was grateful the kids had Ted's plan. *Well, there's a plus for Ted, for once.*

"But how are you? It looks like you're thriving here, sis."

"Honestly, so busy. So worried. So overwhelmed. But you know what? I'm doing pretty good. I'm also so happy." Ali loved being busy. She loved a project, and for the first time ever, she was the boss, not the person who had to give credit to the boss.

"How's that handsome Henry?"

"Oh, well, I'm not divorced yet, so I'm trying to keep my head."

"You know, I don't know about that. I think you're owed some good grown-up time with Henry after what Ted has put you through."

"Stop. You're owed some vacation time after that drive. I insist that you relax when you're here. Period."

Ali knew that Faye would do no such thing, but she was going to at least try to get her baby sister to take care of herself.

Twelve

ALI

Ali was used to doing things on her own. She was the oldest daughter, the manager of Frogtown, and the perennial big sister. She was self-sufficient to a fault. She wasn't used to help, but help seemed to find her all the time here in Haven Beach.

She'd borrowed Jorge's truck and picked up a dozen new lounge chairs for the pool area. She purposely did not tell Faye or Sawyer about her project, she knew they'd feel obligated to leave their spots on the beach and come with her.

It didn't occur to her that someone else might help her load them, unload them, put them together, arrange them.

She didn't expect concierge service. She didn't expect to be babied. She never had been, even with Ted. He didn't particularly like doing any manual labor. Ali didn't mind manual labor. She was Bruce Kelly's daughter, after all.

When she backed into the parking lot of The Sea Turtle and started unloading the lounge chairs, one by one, she didn't expect —or even want—Henry's help.

But there he was, ready and willing to lend her some of his long, lean muscle. Did he know in her book this was better than a dozen roses? Helping her with chores?

"Don't you have a restaurant to run?" Ali said.

"Hey, I'm the boss. If I can't knock off early to put together chairs for my neighbor, what's this about?" Henry teased.

"How did you even know?"

"I have my sources; they're instructed to alert me when I can show up and seem heroic. But I can't reveal them, and have it ruin my mystique."

She knew very well who the sources were: Didi and Jorge. No doubt in her mind about that.

"I'm used to having a staff of convention custodians and mechanics and even Teamsters. I'm not easily impressed, you realize."

"Fine then, I'll carry two lounges at a time and suck in my gut while doing that. So there."

Henry did not have a gut, but he made her laugh a lot. Working on a project with him didn't seem like work at all.

The two of them unpacked the six new lounge chairs and arranged them around the pool.

"Hey, this looks a lot better," Henry said, admiring the nearly clear water.

"Right? A few busted tiles, but at least it looks like a pool and not a bog," said Ali.

"Shame, those tiles are vintage, probably never going to find a match."

Pool tiles would have to go on her never-ending list.

The pool had been looking swampy when she first visited. Now Silvio, the pool guy, had been working hard, and Jorge had been monitoring the pH and chlorine levels like a NASA scientist. It did Ali's heart good to know that she actually did have a guy—actually, a couple of guys—in Haven Beach, even though she was a newbie. A pool guy, a maintenance guy, and a hot guy, or whatever Henry was.

For a second, that thought gave her a flash of her dad. He was the handy guy. She'd call him for leaks and weird malfunctions and repairs. In her early journey as a homeowner, he'd come over, and they'd fix whatever it was together. They bonded over DIY projects. Bruce Kelly wasn't one to talk about emotions or life events, but finding the right washer to go on the right screw? Well, he could talk your ear off.

Later, he'd "supervise" her efforts or whatever contractor she'd hired. Managing this property would have been such a great fit for him.

Why had he hidden this? It was a question that recycled to the front of her mind anytime something made her think of Bruce Kelly.

Ali shook it off and tried to remember to enjoy this moment, this task, this "guy" who was helping her get this new dream off the ground.

As they put the last of the lounges together, the sun set over the water. They had missed the Grand Finale, tonight, but there was still work to be done. Soon enough, when the guests arrived, Henry, Erica, and Ali would be on the beach every evening, watching the sunset with the vacationers. It was a perk, Didi said, that topped just about all the work you had to do to manage the resort.

Ali could add Faye and Sawyer to that group, too! The thought of her family being here lightened her melancholy about her dad. She'd done a lot of work, and there was more to do, but she'd never shied away from work, and she had family here now. That, and looking at the way the pool area was coming together, gave Ali a sense of accomplishment and hope.

Henry sat down on one of the lounges and patted the one next to him. Ali joined him. They kicked their feet up and enjoyed the fruits of their labor for a moment.

"I never understand why this place has a pool when the ocean is right there," Henry said.

Ali explained, "Sometimes the ocean can be a little bit intimidating for the little ones, and the pool is a nice break."

"True. And I mean, we could get a red flag or even a red tide day...or week...heck, even a red tide two weeks."

Ali did not want to think about that. Losing a whole week or two—or worse, a season—could really cut into her business plans. She brushed it off. That would be part of the long-term planning: dealing with the environment, dealing with the uncertain nature of weather, surf, bacteria—and God forbid, oil. Life at the beach was a little bit more than just mimosas. She knew she would learn, and she also knew every day, every season, would bring new challenges. That was part of the adventure!

The two of them sat for a few minutes, letting their aching muscles relax.

"Well, I guess you're right. I should get back to the restaurant," Henry said.

"You know, you've just done so much for me. I don't know what I'd do without you," Ali replied.

Ali was too old to hold back appreciation for people in her life. She was free with compliments and gratitude. She managed the Frogtown that way, and now, here, it was even more important to let her small circle know she saw what they were helping her build.

Henry put out his hand beside her lounge. She placed her hand in his. It felt natural. It felt like maybe it was time to go to the next level with this person, who she now admitted to herself she was powerfully attracted to. Though being attracted to one of the most eligible bachelors this side of Tampa Bay did not seem like a great idea.

Get in line, Ali; everyone thinks Henry is dreamy.

But somehow, Henry seemed to want to spend time with her, and not the young beach beauties that walked up and down the sand all day.

"Doing work with you isn't like doing work," he said. "It's like doing life."

Ali smiled, and her heart melted. She felt the same. She took one of his hands and placed it on her face. She lifted her chin, and for the first time in forever, she let someone kiss her who wasn't her husband.

Inside, it felt no different than being a teenager. Ali felt a thrill from her toes to her earlobes.

When their lips separated, Henry said, "Wow."

"That was...probably the best thing you could say. I'm way out of practice with kissing people other than my ex or soon-to-be exhusband."

Uh oh, what am I saying?

Ali was concerned she had ruined it. But Henry smiled, making it almost impossible to remain embarrassed. He accepted her awkward pauses and made them somehow less awkward.

"I know where you are right now. I'm in no hurry. I know how strange it is to go from one life to another. You're still doing that...I'll wait...unless you don't want me to wait," Henry added, waggling his eyebrows.

Ali was glad the sun had gone down because she could feel her cheeks flush. She was still new to the whole flirting-with-a-handsome-man scenario. She thought it best to stand up, walk away, and take things slowly. Waiting felt like the way to go, for now.

He stood up, too, but this time, they held hands and walked together toward the courtyard of The Sea Turtle.

That's when all hell broke loose—when the man she'd left in Toledo showed up in the courtyard at The Sea Turtle Resort.

Thirteen

FAYE

"Mom, I can't believe we're not staying at The Sea Turtle."

The moment she took him away from the beach and to their lovely little hotel suite, Sawyer wilted like a flower that hadn't been watered in months.

"Sawyer, Aunt Ali has a lot to deal with, much less dealing with us staying at The Sea Turtle. Those rooms aren't ready for us. Plus, I've got bonus points to use."

Sawyer dumped his backpack on the floor of his room.

They had two rooms and an efficiency kitchen—enough to keep them out of Ali's hair but close enough that they could walk to The Sea Turtle. Faye thought it was the perfect scenario. Sawyer, though, had turned into a beach bum overnight and appeared to be having an allergic reaction to hotel points and free WiFi.

"Look, we don't need fancy. You don't need fancy. I don't need fancy. We could help more if we were there," Sawyer said.

He was surprisingly willing to work when it came to The Sea Turtle. But every time she brought up college, he seemed to have a ready reason to change the subject. Work when it came to college? Well, that was a non-starter, apparently.

He'd agreed to a deal where he would go back to OSU after spring break and finish out the year, but that also meant finishing his registration for classes, buying books, and doing other things that he conveniently didn't have time for.

What he did have time for was a newfound appreciation for the beach.

"Look, I'm gonna walk over there, okay?

"Fine, fine."

She'd brought him to Haven Beach to see the beach. Faye didn't want to be a killjoy or spend their brief time there worrying over her wayward son in the sun. As a single mom, she was always the one to put the kibosh on, well, everything. Faye took a breath and tried to reset. Their future was unsure right now. Sawyer had no path, and really, neither did she.

Admittedly, she would also rather be at The Sea Turtle helping Ali get breakfasts and Grand Finales ready than here. Faye was itching to get her hands on the plants that grew wildly all over the property.

"I'll see you soon. Listen, don't get in Ali's way, OK?"

"I'm gonna do whatever she needs. I can clean the pool, there's a beach, I can rake things, I can paint things—she won't know what to do without me!" Sawyer winked at her.

How did she get so lucky to have this kid? Oh wait, she knew, it was constant vigilance.

"Good, glad to hear it!"

Faye did believe him. Sawyer may have the look of a beach bum, but he was a problem solver. Tell him to pick something up and move it somewhere else. He could do that. Ask him to put together a bookshelf, he was on it. He wasn't lazy, so why had college been such a drama?

Her worries threatened to darken their sunny first day in Florida. That thought had her calling after her son headed for the sun.

"Make sure to put on some sunscreen."

"Mom, you know me. I don't get sunburned."

He walked out the door and down Gulf Boulevard. It was a short distance to The Sea Turtle, and that was good.

And he did get sunburned. He just didn't know it yet. The young person who had been slathered with sunscreen from head to toe by their mother their entire life was going to get a rude awakening in Florida. The Florida sun was nothing like Toledo's.

Still, helping Ali was a better focus than fretting over Sawyer's entire future. Today, at least, he was focused and had a plan. Helping Ali.

She wanted the same.

Faye had decided, based on what she had seen at The Sea Turtle, that she could help her sister with some landscaping. Between interior renovations, the swimming pool, and the million other things Ali was doing, the foliage around the resort was looking overgrown, unkempt, and slightly terrifying. Faye had plans; she was going to whip the landscaping into shape while she was in Haven Beach.

A Google search showed that the big-box stores were too much of a haul to get to, but there was a local garden center she had her eye on.

Faye would buy some sort of mulch material, a rake, and garden gloves. It was her mission, over the time they were there, to get the grounds of The Sea Turtle looking, if not perfect, at least not like an overgrown jungle.

With Sawyer gone it was as good a time as any to get cracking on supplies.

She drove two miles to the garden center she'd found with her online search.

When she walked in, she felt like she'd gone to green thumb heaven.

Fourteen

ALI

Ali and Henry walking hand in hand was a big step and not one she was willing to be "Facebook Official" about, much less reveal to her daughter—who she'd just walked smack dab into!

Katie Harris stepped back and stood on the pool deck, mouth open, eyes wide like she'd seen a sea monster. Her arms dangled next to her. She shook her head from side to side.

"Mom, what are you doing?"

Ali had not been doing anything, but all of a sudden, she felt that teenager feeling again. This time, it was not in a good way. Katie Harris, her nearly all grown up college-aged daughter, all five-feet-seven of her lanky self, looked a lot like Bruce Kelly in that moment. She'd been caught! With a boy!

"What am *I* doing? What are *you* doing here? You didn't tell me you were coming, and I'm so happy to see you!!" She was. She'd been excited to see Faye, and now here was Katie, albeit the worst side of Katie, the side that was Daddy's little girl.

"Mom, get it together. Dad is in the parking lot with the bags, and he's practically right behind me."

"Wait, what?"

Her daughter looked Henry up and down and then called back.

"Dad! Found her, we're back here, and Mom's out here with some, uh, guy."

Katie could be terrifying. She was a mini-Ali, people used to say: all boss, all efficiency, all grown up, even as a toddler. But right now, Ali was wishing her uber-mature girl would dial it down a notch or three.

"Excuse me, don't be rude, Katie. This is my friend, Henry."

"Your friend, okay, sure. I'm not going to tell Dad you were holding hands with your *friend*."

Ali had shielded Katie from the details of the breakup of the marriage. She didn't want to be the one who showed her daughter that Ted was a cad. After all, did being a bad husband mean he wasn't a good dad? Ali thought the two things could be separate. But right now, she was questioning that logic. Right now, her daughter appeared to be looking very much at Ali as the "bad guy" in the current family situation. Ted had cheated but now Ali looked like the loose woman in the equation. She did not like that feeling one bit.

"Honey, I'm so glad you're here, but what's going on? What's happening?"

"Look, it's spring break. I wanted to come down. I know Sawyer is here, and Aunt Faye. Dad said there's a ton of room here, and uh, Dad...well..." Katie paused and then lowered her voice to a whisper. "Dad needs you, plus he wouldn't let me drive here on my own."

For that, at least, Ali was grateful. She didn't like the idea of Katie on the I-75 by herself for twenty hours.

"What do you mean he needs me, honey? The papers are almost all set. I know that this is a huge change, but—" Ali had more to say, more words of reassurance to dole out, but before she could, her serial philandering soon-to-be-ex-husband, the man with whom she'd built a life with until a few weeks ago, walked around the corner and onto the pool patio.

It was Ted, but also not Ted. He looked different. He was almost gaunt.

"Ali, hello!" Ted smiled. He was embarrassed, demure almost, in contrast to Katie barging right in. "I'm sorry, Katie wanted to surprise you. I told her we should give you a heads-up. You know our daughter, she gets an idea, and the rest of the planet just needs to get out of the way."

This was a phrase they'd said about their girl since the moment she pulled herself up on the side of the crib and then jumped out!

Katie and Ted were always close, and she was Daddy's little girl, but the vibe between them right now was strained. It was strained between all three of them. This part of Ali's life had been on the backburner from the moment she put her toes in the sand. It was now smacking her in the face.

She knew Ted had sold his stupid sports car. She knew Ted had to take a few days off from the university for mental health or something like that. But she had tried not to get sucked into the stories that Katie was telling her. *Ted. Ted. Ted.* Ted was an adult and should take care of himself. This wasn't her problem.

But what Ali could see, when she looked from Katie to Ted, was that he'd been making their daughter step in. Katie was taking care of Ted and not the other way around.

A wave of guilt washed over Ali. She never wanted her kids to be in the position she'd been in. Ali knew all too well that when the mother wasn't there, the eldest daughter was the next one at-bat to clean up the messes.

Katie was cleaning up Ted's messes. It made her furious to think her girl was being asked to deal with her immature father. That wasn't fair to Katie. Ali wanted to be done with Ted, and she thought she was done with Ted. But here he was, leaning on Katie and showing up on her doorstep!

Thoughts ran through her mind: where to put them, what to do next. Meanwhile, her—

Henry, uh, just Henry—was there, enjoying this moment of awkwardness brought to you by legal separation. Divorce, it's what's for dinner.

"Henry, this is Ted and Katie."

"Nice to meet you both, I hate to be rude, but I do need to get back to the restaurant." Henry nodded at Ali's family and gave her a wink that only she could see.

He got out of there. Ali would too, if she could. But even here, there was no escape hatch.

Ted was here, and so was Katie. They expected to find a bed, and they expected Ali to take care of all of them. Her "vacation" was over.

Fifteen

DIDI – 1990

"I have something to tell you. Something bad."

"Didi, if you tell me you're a serial killer, I'd be okay with it. That's how much I love you."

Jorge Rivera was perfect in every way. They'd been married for a month after dating for a year, and so far, so good. Didi didn't know what she'd done to deserve to find true love this late in the game, but she was grabbing it with both hands.

She'd almost told Jorge three times before, during their engagement. But she hadn't wanted to scare him away.

It turned out he was unscareable.

Things with her sister were frostier than she'd like them to be. They had another fight over The Sea Turtle and the girls.

Didi had snuck away to Toledo right before her wedding. Joetta refused to go. Joetta's life had raced in a totally different direction than Toledo, Ohio.

"Just tell Banks it's a Gulfside Girls shopping weekend," Didi suggested, offering Joetta a plausible cover story.

"I'm sorry. I can't. And I don't think you should anymore, either."

Didi had been back to Toledo an average of once a year. For her, the mission was clear: make sure her nieces are okay. Well fed. Healthy. She wanted to find something, anything that would justify her stepping in and taking them with her back to Florida.

Once, she saw Ali pushing little Blair on a swing with Faye jumping off another swing, over and over. They all were laughing. Their cheeks were rosy. Their eyes sparkled. There was nothing wrong with them. At all.

On another trip, she'd gone to a Christmas play for the girls' school. She sat in the back. Stayed in the shadows.

She even saw Bruce Kelly in the audience. He wasn't laughing or sparkling. But he was there, and he clapped for the girls.

Her last trip found her on the periphery of their day at school. It was a field day, and the girls were all in various events. She watched Ali in a relay race, Faye in a throwing contest, and Blair on a tricycle obstacle course.

Didi was in a full-throated laugh when a teacher came over to her.

"Are you a mom? Who's little ones are yours?" In all her previous spying, Didi had never been approached. But the teacher's question was innocent.

Didi pointed to a little boy who was blowing bubbles at one of the field day stations.

"Oh, little Jeremy, so sweet."

No sooner had the teacher gotten that out than Didi slid out of sight. She was going to get caught if she kept it up. Heck, she'd probably get arrested for stalking little kids!

She wasn't going to be able to do this much longer. Her concern for the girls was genuine, and she'd learned that Bruce Kelly might have been a terrible husband, but he was a good father. The girls were cared for. Didi knew that she had zero rights to them or really any reason to check in on them anymore.

It was that last trip that actually did get her caught by Jorge. He'd seen her credit card statement and asked why she'd flown to Toledo, Ohio, of all places.

And so, she told him.

Jorge was as shocked as anyone would be. She told him she hoped he didn't think she was a monster for doing this.

"They aren't your kids. And you're trying your best to make sure they're okay. When this all gets sorted out, it will be Joetta who's got to answer for the lie."

"What about Bruce?" Didi wondered who was to blame after all these years.

"Him too, but I see that you're not the one who put this together. You're only trying to be a good aunt and a good big sister."

"And wife. You're not leaving me after hearing my worst secret?"

"No, but I do wonder what kind of person your sister is."

"She's trying her best. Bruce didn't give her a choice. Except we do have that resort to run, and I'm committed to keeping it alive as long as I can, so they can inherit it or get a little nest egg from it at least."

"I'll help you."

For the first time, Didi had a person to trust with her secret. And a person who could shoulder some of the responsibilities of The Sea Turtle.

Jorge lightened the load she was carrying, and she loved him for that, and a million other things.

Sixteen

ALI

Ali looked at her daughter and her soon-to-be ex-husband.

How in the world did he think it was okay to show up here?

They weren't in the post-marriage "now we're friends" stage, not by a mile.

They were in the "you are pond scum, and I don't want to look at you ever again" stage.

Well, she was in that stage, anyway.

Every email exchange had been terse, and every call worse. Ali's lawyer had told her to refer all communications to the firm, but it was hard to do that. It was hard to turn a foundational relationship into a transactional one. They hadn't signed the papers yet, but the papers were ready to go.

Reminding herself what she'd learned too late, that Ted was a cheater, helped Ali stop taking calls, helped her shift conversations away from him when Katie called, and helped her move on here, at Haven Beach.

Up until showing up by the pool, Ted had said of the resort, "You're gambling our children's inheritance with this scheme."

"The scheme." That's what he called The Sea Turtle and her plan to run it and not liquidate it. They couldn't be divorced soon enough.

But here she was in front of her daughter and Ted, and she didn't want a scene. She didn't want to fight with Ted, and she hadn't told Katie why the marriage was over.

How do you tell your kids the worst thing about their dad? She didn't know where she stood on preserving her children's relationship with their father, so she hadn't done a thing to explain herself.

She could see now that she'd made herself the bad guy in this trio. Because Katie didn't know the worst, she assumed Ali was the bolter, the one who'd bailed on their family.

She put on her most diplomatic expression. Ali didn't want to say something now that she couldn't take back. *Stay cool, stay cool*, she repeated in her mind.

She looked at Ted again, really looked at him. She noticed that he looked different. He was thinner. He looked older. He seemed tired. Maybe he really didn't know how to take care of himself. She made his doctor's appointments, she filled his prescriptions, and she reminded him to have a colonoscopy. She did all that, and he did anything in a skirt, apparently.

Her vows flashed in her head; vows she'd taken seriously. She had promised to take care of Ted in sickness and health. He looked sick, and she knew she looked healthy, better than she'd looked in years, thanks to the sea air, she thought.

Ali was also a mother. It shouldn't be Katie's job to take care of Ted. Her college-aged daughter was doing the job Ali should do: deal with Ted.

Ali opened her heart, let down her guard, and asked Ted, "How are you doing?"

"Not great, but surviving, barely," Ted said.

He was so different now than he'd been in their terse

exchanges. In their last argument over selling this place, he looked broken. *Was it possible that I broke his heart?* She dismissed that thought. *Nope. Not possible.*

"Mom, Dad almost died." Katie looked at her as though it was her fault that Ted "almost died."

"Yeah, what happened?"

"Well, your daughter's grades are slipping. Perhaps we should talk about that?" Ted looked at Katie, their four-point-oh honors student.

"Dad, tell her about the car. And your condition." Katie looked from Ted to Ali.

"The car?" She was sick to death of Ted's sports car, and she'd dumped a bag of dirt in it on her way out the door.

"Well, I had an allergic reaction to the mold in the soil, which was in the heating vents, and—oh, it's not important. I'm on the mend."

"Pretty juvenile move, Mom, dumping that dirt because Dad wouldn't let you use the garage."

That was not why she did it. She did it because "dad" was privately "tutoring" a co-ed.

But Ali stayed quiet.

Katie was clearly at the end of her rope with her dad. However, a twenty-hour drive could test any relationship. Ali ignored the barbs from her daughter.

"Honey, why don't you go take a walk on the beach? It's right there. It's gorgeous. I'm going to figure out what to do with both of you. I hate to say it, but I haven't got a lot of room around here."

"Mom, please."

Her daughter, despite all the attitude, was really still her baby girl. The answer was going to be yes, yes, of course her girl could stay. But Ted? That was another story.

"Well, but they're not all fixed up. I wanted you to see the final product, not the work in progress."

"I don't need it fancy, I just—" Katie started to cry.

What in the world? Ali rushed forward. She gathered her daughter in her arms. "Honey, it's OK. I've got you. It's fine."

She looked over Katie's head toward Ted. He looked more like someone who needed help than someone who was sleeping his way through Northwest Ohio.

"OK, let's figure this out. I'm going to put you in the Blueberry with me."

Ali had the room in the cottages and the inn. That was true. And if Ted weren't there, she'd have been thrilled to see Katie and have her stay. Ted's presence put a dampener on the great feelings she had about seeing her daughter.

"Listen, I don't need anything fancy either. I'm pretty tired. All I need is a bed and a bathroom."

Ted was trying, she could see, to be accommodating. After months of adversarial stances with her husband, here he was, to some degree, with a less aggressive attitude.

It was only a week. And she did have room, loads of it right now. Thanks to only having two bookings.

"Okay." The awkwardness faded a bit. Ted could be in the inn. She didn't even need to see him if he was there. Ali couldn't shake the thought that they had been a family for more than half her life. "Let's head to the office. I have keys and little maps." She loved the little maps she'd created to hand out to guests, just like the big resorts.

She led them both to the office. She'd made some organizational improvements since she'd first set foot in it. But she still had a place for Jorge and Didi. In fact, they had more space since she'd computerized the bookings, the inventory, and the schedule.

In Ali's mind, there would always be a place for Jorge and Didi. A place for Ted? This was a bit harder. Ali found a spare set of keys for the Blueberry. She knew what state it was in—

not updated but clean. Kitschy was the vibe there and she

hoped Katie liked it. She'd selected for herself while she worked. Soon, though, she'd rent it out; well, she hoped she would.

She handed them the cute little maps. Neither of them commented. It bummed her out a bit. She'd *ooh* and *ahh* over Ted's papers, of course, and all her kids' artwork, but they didn't see her work. Maybe they didn't see her.

"Hang out a minute, okay, while I get Katie sorted? Take a load off, do a load of laundry."

"Oh, that's what those things are, washers and dryers," Ted said.

She wished he was joking. "Ha ha." Ali couldn't help it. Ted had never done a single load of laundry when they lived together. She wondered now if he managed it.

Ali helped Katie with her bags, and they walked through the courtyard to the Blueberry. The sound of the ocean waves calmed her, and she saw Katie pause and take it in as well.

"I'm still not used to how great that sound is. It always lightens my mood, you'll see."

"Yeah, I can't wait to get in the sand tomorrow."

She unlocked the Blueberry and let Katie inside.

Each of the cottages had two rooms. She had her stuff in the master, so the second room would be Katie's for the week.

"It's so weird to me, staying with you. And dad is staying somewhere else."

"I know it's going to take a while for all of this to feel normal. Why didn't you tell me you needed so much help with your dad?"

"Well, at first, he didn't want me to tell you, but then lately, it's gotten worse. He seems to think I should do his laundry, clean the house, and do my classes. I don't live there, but it's like I do, the amount he's been bugging me."

"I haven't heard from Tye in a couple of weeks. Is your dad bugging him too?"

"No, because Tye is a—"

"Boy." They said it together. For an over-educated professor,

Ted Harris could be positively medieval when it came to household chores.

"I just...I just can't deal with it anymore."

"Well, how about you spend the week getting some sun, enjoying the beach, getting ready for next semester?"

"I don't want to drop out of college. I just...I just threatened that to get Dad's attention."

"It's a pretty good threat. Are your grades doing all right?"

"Yeah, I'm still pulling a 3.5 for the semester. Dad's just been, well, a lot. And you, leaving. I mean, I don't get it. I get you're allowed to do what you want, but it's not the same at home."

"I'm sorry."

She hugged her girl. Ali would make this right, and she knew how to ease the burden, at least for this week.

"I can see that your dad needs some help. I'll do what I can. I'm glad you're here, honey. The shower's over here. That whole room is yours. You're going to love it."

"I already do love it. It's great. You know, I think it's 22° in Toledo right now," Katie said.

She'd leave her daughter to organize her things. Katie was a neat freak, and sometimes, when Ali saw Katie stress over a detail, she felt a twinge of guilt. They were the same in that way.

But now it was time to talk to Ted. She didn't want Ted there. She didn't want to put Ted up, but it was hard to argue the fact that she didn't have room. She had a lot of room; they just weren't luxurious or ready for the public.

Ted had waited in the office. She walked in, and he finished some sort of phone call.

"Talk to you later. Thanks, bye."

"All right, Ted. Our daughter is going to stay with me. That makes sense. I'm thrilled actually to have her. Seriously, what's going on with you?"

"I know you don't have any reason to want to help me, but it has been rough."

"You know, you cheated on me for decades, and I finally caught you. So, I don't think it's my job to take care of you. Or Katie's job."

"I haven't asked you to."

"You showed up here. Katie seems to think you're not able to handle your life without her or me."

"I'm uh, it's fine."

Ted was trying to be stoic? *This is new.*

"I don't know what the right thing to say is, Ted. We're almost done. We've got the papers. Why can't we just sign them?"

"Sure, honestly, I just didn't want Katie to drive down here all by herself. She was going to do that, and I just didn't think it was a good idea. I'm still on leave, so, well, I guess I didn't think it all through. Whatever you think, I have been out of it since all this started."

"I am grateful you drove with her. I don't like the idea of her driving cross-country alone, either. We've got plumbing going and electricity in the inn next door. But there's no mini-fridge or..." She stopped herself. "You're sure you don't want to head over to the local Marriott? I promise you it's nicer."

"I'm good here. Thank you."

"Fine. Let me grab the keys."

She grabbed the keys to the first-floor room at The Sea Turtle Inn. The Sea Turtle was the long-term plan. Someday, they would have every room at The Sea Turtle filled and every cottage and resort occupied all year. But right now, they were all empty because they were all kind of a mess.

She walked him over to the inn. Ali opened the door to Room 101 and let Ted in. She was almost disappointed they didn't find a gecko on the bed or a spider in the shower, but even so, Ted's reaction wasn't unexpected.

"Oh, wow. Yikes."

"Well, I told you it wasn't the Ritz."

"No, no, it's great. This is great. I appreciate it. You're doing a great job here. I can't wait to see it in the daytime."

"Sure."

"Who is that guy?"

For a moment, she was thrown off. *Guy? What guy? Oh, yeah, Henry.*

"He's my friend."

And that was the end of the conversation that Ali wanted to have.

"There's no room service," she told Ted. "The phone doesn't work, and there's no breakfast. I'm too busy to entertain you and Katie can entertain herself."

"Sure."

Ali closed the door and walked back toward the cottages. She had no idea what she felt. On the one hand, she wanted to help her daughter. On the other, she wanted more time to get this new life underway. Having her old life here, even a little, felt like a bit of a setback.

When she got back to the Blueberry, Katie was ensconced in the room, headphones on, face in phone. One thing she had learned about being a girl mom was that girls came to you when they wanted, not when you wanted.

"I'm turning in," she said to her daughter.

Katie nodded.

Ali normally slept deeply with the sea breeze lulling her into her dreams. That night, she tossed and turned. She dreamed she was in a car with Ted, and he was going the wrong way down a one-way street. She yelled, but Ted didn't hear her.

Seventeen

FAYE

The Mangrove Garden Grotto was the funkiest, most magical nursery and garden supply store Faye had ever seen.

Faye walked into the place like a five-year-old walking down Main Street of the Magic Kingdom. Her eyes were wide, and her head was on a slow swivel.

Plants, flowers, tools, pottery, a neon sign on any available wall, tent roofing, trellises, and an artful array of everything green you could imagine. It seemed to spring from Faye's dreams and into reality. It was slightly bohemian and almost seemed like a jungle rather than a retail store, but large scripted signage let her know where to go in the space to find perennials, annuals, herbs, fertilizer, supplies and garden art.

They even had a gardening gift shop, and she almost bought herself a t-shirt that said "Hoeing Ain't Easy." But she realized she'd be the only one who got it. No one in her family had the same love of growing as she did.

Faye could have been there all day, and after hours of

wandering the aisles and loading cart after cart, she realized she nearly *had* been there all day. She'd meant to do a quick trip, but instead, she'd wandered, grabbed plants, wandered again, and grabbed still more.

She'd piled one or two tools into her cart while she was at it. Faye figured Jorge probably had a pretty good complement of tools in the shed at the resort, but she didn't want to impose or assume.

After grabbing a few more essentials she'd then found herself walking through the aisles of flats of flowers.

What must it be like to live in this zone where you could grow almost all year? It seemed like a dream. She'd been in Northwest Ohio her entire life. The growing season really only lasted from Mother's Day until early October if you didn't have a greenhouse. She really wanted a greenhouse, but her yard was tiny.

Her neighbor, Mr. Moore, was going to water the seedlings she had started before they left—lettuce, onions, and peppers. But she only had a small window in Toledo, nothing like this place.

Faye's plants were almost as important to her as Sawyer. She loved growing them and, a lot of times, understood them a heck of a lot better than she understood her man/child son.

Plants grew, plants could be thinned, they could be replanted. Water, soil, sun; those were the variables. Plants didn't wilt at Ohio State for no discernable reason. If she could add water or fertilizer to him, it would be a lot easier.

There was no doubt her overriding concern these days was Sawyer's future, not gardening, but somehow, in this space, she got lost in a good way. The worry about Sawyer's aimless future took a backseat for a moment.

She wound up deciding on bringing a few plants home to The Sea Turtle. Of course, the main issue was overgrowth there, but a few potted plants right by the front office would be gorgeous. Then she started thinking about the pool. She assessed the Lantana, Hibiscus, the Bougainvillea. It was too hard to say no to any of them. It was an actual effort to get out of there.

Faye had to get to work and stop wandering the Grotto like a garden zombie!

She got to the car and realized her Jeep—while an SUV—certainly wasn't going to be big enough for all the stuff she had just bought.

Faye reshuffled. She wondered if some could fit on her lap and generally scratched her head at how she'd gone from a quick trip for a few things to this load she was itching to plant.

"Hey, looks like your eyes were bigger than your stomach." A very broad, very bald, very tan man wearing a Garden Grotto t-shirt approached her in the parking lot.

After her recent encounter at the rest stop, Faye was wary of anybody in parking lots. But the t-shirt with the funky logo to match the one on the wall of the Grotto assuaged her fears. This was an employee, not a rest-stop creeper.

"Yeah, darn it. I didn't really think about how I was going to get it all out of here. I got excited buying plants for 10b," she said, placing one flat next to another flat, turning a flat sideways. But the more she worked, the more dirt started to spill out all over the Jeep.

"Well, actually, if you're planting all this in Haven Beach, it's 11a."

"Wow, really, that's the average minimum temp of what? 40 to 45 instead of 35 to 40?"

"Impressive, you know your zones. That ten-degree swing is a big factor."

"I bet." Faye was recalculating her plants and positions. 11a. Okay, she could work with that!

"Where are you headed?"

"The Sea Turtle. Do you know it?"

"Oh, definitely. I love The Sea Turtle. Love Jorge and Didi. A friend of mine was out there the other day doing some work."

"Yeah, my sister is the new owner—although she was really the old owner, but that's a story for a different day."

"Oh, awesome. So, you are...?"

"I'm Faye. I'm trying to help her get the landscaping together."

"Yeah, Didi and Jorge used to handle a lot, but they are getting on a little. I'm sure there's a bit of work there."

"Yeah, they are. And there is."

"Hey, you know what? All this stuff will fit in my truck, no problem. How about this? Whatever's left over, I'll put in my truck and bring it over this evening after I close up shop."

"You don't have to do that. I can just make two trips."

"My pleasure. I'd love to see what you've got in mind. I haven't been to The Sea Turtle in years. I used to go to the Grand Finale now and again, but..." He trailed off.

Faye had been to a couple of Grand Finales on the beach during her last visit. Apparently, the event was locally famous.

"I can't let you do that; I'm the one who misjudged my towing capacity."

"I'll just bring all this stuff with me this evening after I'm done here. Any friend of Didi and Jorge is a friend of mine."

"Wow, okay. I'm sorry, I didn't catch your name?"

"Rudy, the name's Rudy Palmer, though sometimes they call me Rudy Palm Tree. Don't hold it against me."

She laughed. *Rudy Palm Tree!*

"Thanks so much, Rudy. Are you sure you're allowed to do special deliveries?"

"The boss likes to have new loyal customers, so I may even get a raise."

"Well, then, I accept."

"Nice to meet a fellow green thumb. I've been known to lose my head in a garden center, too."

"What?"

"I saw you wandering around. Plants. You were in another world."

Faye was embarrassed. She'd probably looked like a loon.

"Oh, gosh, yeah. Sometimes I forget the time when I'm with green stuff."

"Well, it may be another world to someone else, but it's in our world, isn't it?" He gave her a wink, closed the hatch of her Jeep, and waved before heading back into the garden center.

That was the nicest garden center worker I've ever met in my life, thought Faye.

But now it really was time to get to work. The Sea Turtle was going to need a lot of TLC, especially if she was only going to be there for a week.

Eighteen

DIDI

Didi and Jorge were back in action. It had taken a while, and sure, they weren't as fast as they used to be, but Ali seemed to like having them around.

Didi's heart nearly exploded with glee as she watched Jorge show Ali where the drill bits were or how to restart the pool heater.

Ali would ask about a repair or need the name of a contractor, and they'd be at the ready with information. Weirdly, a lot of their people were retiring, but still, they were a good resource, and it was clear that Ali appreciated having them.

The notion that this place would live on after them, someday, put joy in Didi's heart. Her own kids had zero interest. But of course, it wasn't theirs anyway. Seeing Jorge in action with Ali and just having her niece in her life, was two dreams come true. Even though she was keeping very quiet about the dream of her family reunited.

Didi's plate was decidedly less full with Ali in charge, and it was good for her arthritis to get to move at a little slower pace. She was going at that slow pace, outside the Mango Mansion—Jorge was working on a leaky showerhead inside—when she spied Sawyer. He really did take her breath away.

If Ali would ever get a look at the old family pictures, she'd know how much Sawyer looked like everyone in the Bennett family tree. Blonde, handsome, and though he was the son of a proud blue-collar mama, his grandfather's profile was there under that mop of hair. It put a little skip in Didi's heartbeat, seeing him. She imagined traveling back in time and catching a glimpse of her own grandfather as a teen on that very beach. She had forgotten what her grandfather's voice sounded like, but something of Sawyer's deep cadence took her back. It was her grandfather who'd bought this land originally, self-made he used to say. She didn't know what that meant back then. She did know now, and it made her proud of her grandfather, and of Jorge.

The way the gene pool flowed through them all warmed her but also terrified her. What if someone else noticed? Then, the story would have to come out.

Still, make no mistake, that kid was made to be on the beach. He was already tan, freckles sprouting on his nose. When Didi caught up with him, he was carrying an Adirondack chair to the array of palm trees that edged the space between the cottages and the beach.

Jorge had asked him to find the chairs and bring them out. The kid was eager and full of energy. His mother claimed he was a slacker and not motivated to work, but every time Didi saw him, Sawyer was lending a hand and looking for the next job. He's asked her a million questions about when the pool was built and spent an inordinate time carefully pulling up a broken tile. *Whatever floats your boat, kid*, is what she'd told him. But today, Didi had a different idea for Sawyer and his boundless beachy energy.

"You know, I wonder," she said to Sawyer.

Sawyer looked at her. "What do you wonder, Miss Didi?"

"I wonder if you can dig a hole in the sand."

"Well, I may be a blonde, but I think I can manage the smarts to dig a hole."

She laughed. It was so nice to have someone young running around the place. The dwindling bookings had made The Sea Turtle practically a ghost town. She loved it when it was full. Ali was making that happen. The new blood meant new things to talk about. Prior to Ali's arrival Jorge and Didi's conversations seemed like endless discussions about medical procedures or what ache or pain had sprung up that night.

These days, they were talking about Sawyer's love of pottery and Ali's love of hotel management software. Whatever that was. I was an invigorating change of pace!

Sawyer didn't creak or complain when he went from a sitting to a standing position. He was able to find things in corners of the storage shed that Didi was quite sure would kill her if she tried to climb up or down to get them.

"So, why do you need me to dig a hole, Miss Didi?" he asked.

She like that too, the Miss Didi thing. Thanks to Faye, his mama, this young man was not comfortable calling his elders by their first names. She'd said, "Call me Didi," but the closest he could manage, to offer his respect, was "Miss Didi." He called Jorge, Mr. Jorge. It was adorable and really a throwback.

Faye had taught her son respect and manners. However, it looked like Faye and Sawyer were not quite on the same page about a lot of other things.

"I think that back here in the storage shed, I have four—well, I used to have four—cabanas," she explained.

"What's a cabana?"

"It's like a mini tent that we can put out on the sand every day for our guests to provide a little shade and comfort."

"Won't the wind blow them away?"

"No, we tie them up at night. I mean, we did lose a few during the last hurricane, but most days, if you tie them up, you're good to go. The problem is getting the posts stuck in the sand—that's where the hole digging comes in."

Sawyer didn't need to be asked twice.

"Where's your mom, by the way?"

"Oh, she's at the garden center, so we'll probably never see her again. She's got a green thumb. But really, I think she's got green from her eyebrows down to her ankles."

Didi laughed again. It was easy to be around this young man, and she was realizing they needed to be around him more often.

"So, what do you guys think of the hotel you're in?" she asked.

"It's corporate fabulous," he replied.

Didi did not miss the eye roll. "Oh yeah?" she said. "How about this: I think you and your mother should come and stay in the penthouse of The Sea Turtle Inn."

"The Sea Turtle has a penthouse?"

"Well, I mean, Frank Sinatra allegedly stayed there once in the '40s."

"Who's Frank Sinatra?" Sawyer asked.

Didi smiled and shook her head. "Old Blue Eyes, the Rat Pack."

"Oh, you mean the ones who starred in, what's it called, Elmo's Fire?"

"No, come on. You help me with these cabanas, and I'll show you the penthouse suite of The Sea Turtle. It's a gas." He took the Rat Pack-era slang in with a smile.

A short while later, Faye showed up with a Jeep full of garden supplies, plants, and what looked like a few hundred pounds of mulch. Sawyer and Didi met her in the parking lot.

"My goodness, did you buy out The Grotto?" Didi asked.

"This is only half of it," Faye replied.

"I've got something to tell you, Mom," Sawyer said.

"Okay," Faye said, eyeing her son suspiciously. "But could you please help me unload these?"

"Yes, but there's a price," he told her.

"What's the price?" Faye asked.

"We're staying here, moving out of the Courtyard Corporate Continental Breakfast Hotel."

"Honey. We do not want to add to Aunt Ali's work."

"There's no adding to her work. I've already cleaned out the space, and Didi already got the towels and the linens. And it's the penthouse or presidential suite, I forget, but it's where a guy named Old Blue Thighs stayed?"

"What? Old Blue thighs?" Faye asked.

"Who's got Blue thighs?" Didi had only been half-listening as she checked out the items that Faye had purchased.

"I have no idea," Faye said.

"Anyway, the point is," Didi added, "we've got the penthouse suite all set for you at The Sea Turtle."

"I'm so confused right now," Faye said.

"We call it the penthouse suite. It's a joke, but we do have a hotel registry signature somewhere around here. Frank Sinatra signed in here in 1949, the first year we were in existence. He played a show in Tampa and stayed here for a couple of days with his wife."

Faye looked at Didi, a little skeptical. "Really?"

"Listen, it's a great set of rooms. There is plenty of room for you and Sawyer. It just needs to be rehabbed like the rest of the hotel. But there's no reason for you to spend money at a hotel when you could stay here for free."

That seemed to perk Faye up. She'd just lost her job; free lodging was a good deal.

"Mom, give me the keys. I'm going to unload the Jeep, and then I'm going to go get our stuff. We're staying here. There's no point in being in Haven Beach without being on Haven Beach."

Faye looked at her son, then at Didi, and seemed to understand the situation. "Fine, we'll stay in the presidential penthouse suite, once frequented by Old Blue Thighs."

Didi laughed at Sawyer's misnaming of The Chairman of the Board.

"Old Blue Thighs. That sounds like what I looked like in shorts before I had my varicose veins stripped," she joked.

Faye was the one laughing this time.

Mission accomplished. Didi had brought one more niece into the fold. Before long, she'd have all three.

Nineteen

FAYE

The penthouse suite was decidedly unpresidential, but Didi was right—it had plenty of room. Sawyer had done a halfway decent job of cleaning it, and my goodness, did it have a view of Haven Beach! It was at the top corner of The Sea Turtle Inn, and two walls were all windows. They looked out to the beach and water.

If it was good enough for Frank, it's good enough for me!

It was still very much a foreign concept that she owned this place or a third of it. You'd think that would make her more at ease about finances, but money was still very much an object. If they sold, they'd have cash on hand; if they didn't, hopefully, there'd be a thriving business that would provide an income. Provided that Ali could make this work.

She thought about Blake and Ted. They seemed to be cut from the same cloth, both wanting the women to cash in their chips and split the pot. Faye was lucky there wasn't a man in her life putting that pressure on her. But still, she was now in a much more precarious financial situation than the day she decided to tell Ali not to sell.

She wasn't sure what was going to happen next. She would have a good income when she was retirement age thanks to her pension plan. The buyout package they gave her, was good enough to give her a little cushion. But that wouldn't last forever. She was also too young to retire at forty-eight. She needed to figure out what to do next. That was swirling around her head with her worry about Sawyer's future. Faye took a deep inhale of the salt air. It helped. *One crisis at a time*, she decided.

This week, she'd help her sister, make sure Sawyer didn't get sunburned, and figure out the rest when they got back home to Toledo.

Regardless, saving $350 a night by not staying at the Courtyard was a pretty good reason to let Sawyer and Didi win that battle.

Faye unpacked a little and realized she really hadn't had a complete tour of The Sea Turtle Inn. She'd seen a first-floor room, and she'd seen the outside, and now this gorgeously positioned set of rooms.

But she wondered how much work it would take to get this place ready to be fully booked. And what did Ali want to charge? All those considerations would, thankfully, be left to her sister. Ali knew they'd need to have this hotel up and running along with the cottages, but Ali was also doing all the work herself, so it was going to take some time.

Faye decided to spend the rest of the afternoon clearing some of the plants crawling all over the walkway from the parking lot to the courtyard. Since that was the main drag, so to speak, of The Sea Turtle Resort, it would be the first impression for the guests. Ali had plenty on her plate, so Faye put on her gardening gloves, grabbed her rake and the garbage bags she'd purchased, and got to work.

Some people took spin classes. Some people did Pilates. Thanks to lifting dirt, raking leaves, and mowing her lawn with her old push mower, Faye felt like she was holding on to some sort of tone and shape. She felt strong, if not young, when she was gardening. And she fit into the same cutoff jeans she'd had since the early aughts.

As she started, the teeth of the rake hit the sandy soil around the walkway. A sense of calm came over her. This was her happy place, whether it be her garden in West Toledo or—it turns out—the courtyard of this funky little resort.

Faye could see how the plants thrived here, even though she had a lot to learn about the climate and what was best. She wanted to do a little cleanup before the second delivery of her shopping spree arrived.

As she worked, a familiar voice—though not a friendly one—drifted into her ear. She didn't mean to eavesdrop but eavesdrop she did. *Was that who it sounded like?*

Faye crept closer and closer to the office, only to find Ali and the snake Ted were deep in conversation. *Ted! What the heck was he doing here?*

"That's perfect. I can see what you like about it," Ted said.

Ali shook her head. "I think it has a lot of potential."

"I think you're right. I mean, I guess my only question is—what are you doing about insurance?" Ted asked.

Ali paused for a moment. Faye leaned in to hear better. Ali knew what to do with insurance. For goodness' sake, Ted sounded so condescending.

"I'm working on that, Ted. Thanks," Ali responded.

"You do know insurance prices for these kinds of places have skyrocketed, the inn alone could be prohibitively costly, thanks to the recent hurricane and then the flooding out in California. Beachfront property is not a great deal when it comes to what you're trying to do, so you're probably going to have to up the rental fees. Although, I can't see people wanting to pay a premium for the more rustic accommodations. I'm not saying rustic is bad, just thinking of the practicalities."

Ali didn't say anything.

That jerk was trying to undermine Ali. He always did that, and Ali just took it. *Well, no way, no how.*

"What are *you* doing here?" Faye said, stepping into the conversation. She likely had a sneer on her face. She hoped she did, actually.

Ted looked at the two sisters. "Your sister has been generous enough to let Katie and I stay for the week."

"What?" Faye's last interaction with Ted had been with him falling all over his new girlfriend and Faye telling him off. That interaction had turned disastrous. She hated this guy.

"Are you kidding me? And you're letting him stay here?" Faye asked.

Ali looked at her sister. "Faye, Ted and I can be adults for Katie."

Faye paused. While it would be great to see Katie, she'd had no idea her niece was planning a trip here this week. Faye realized she'd been a crappy aunt along with a bad mother lately. Her job situation had turned her inward. Well, that stopped now. She was going to get involved—big time!

But Ali's tone let her know she might have to do it outside of Ali's earshot. Ali did not like to argue. She wanted everything to be nice for everyone all the time. It was nearly pathological.

Faye did not want things nice for Ted. Plus, she had just witnessed Ted undermine Ali's management in one quick conversation. And, of course, he was acting like he was trying to help her.

"How long are you staying?" Faye asked.

"I guess the same time that you're staying, spring break," Ted said.

"Oh, great. Well, I'll be outside," Faye muttered.

Faye left Ali and Ted to continue their old established pattern: Ted acting way smarter than everyone else in the room and Ali quietly proving herself as the actual brains of the operation. It drove Faye crazy to think her sister believed even one word out of Ted's mouth.

Faye took out her annoyance at Ted on the gravel in the court-yard. The gravel did not stand a chance, she'd decided. It was looking somewhat better after she'd worked about an hour on the front walk.

That's when she heard the gravel crunch—well, more like the sand and shell bits crunch. She really was not used to the media here. Faye looked up and saw the Rudy Palm Tree. She smiled.

Her new plants would be another good distraction from Ted.

"I've got the rest of your plants," he said.

Wow. He's cute. Uh. Handsome. Men are handsome, and boys are cute, she corrected herself.

"Looking pretty good," Faye responded, smiling at him.

Rudy got out of the truck and headed toward her. He filled out that Mangrove Garden Grotto t-shirt pretty well for an old guy. Although noticing dudes in t-shirts wasn't her normal pastime, she was sort of on vacation.

"I can't wait to get my hands on these," she said.

"Where are you thinking?" he asked.

"Well, I was thinking I could put these right here, just in pots along the pool deck. Let me show you."

The two of them did a mini tour of The Sea Turtle.

"Man, I used to come here with my friends. I'm so glad to see you guys are fixing it up," said Rudy.

She and Rudy spent an hour looking at the landscaping, talking about the angles of the sun, and immersing themselves in ideas about how to turn The Sea Turtle into something even more gorgeous than it was before.

Yes, it was the perfect distraction from Ted.

Twenty

ALI

The last three days with her sister and ex and nephew and daughter all over the grounds were a mixed blessing.

On the plus side, Faye was a beast—a literal landscaping tornado.

You could now see the doors and deck areas on each of the cottages. The pathway that led to the entrance of the The Sea Turtle Inn was not only pruned back from all the foliage, but Faye had also scored little solar walkway lighting and lined every path. You could walk from the parking area to the office, from the office into the courtyard, to each little entry of the cottages, to the pool, and up to the doors of the inn easily and safely, and it was all well-lit. Tripping and falling was a liability, after all. Thanks to Ted, she has been thinking about liability a lot more lately.

The lights were genius because they had motion detectors. They turned off right away so that the turtles wouldn't be confused. Faye had made it so the only hazard you could possibly encounter was a gecko crossing. Even though they weren't danger-ous, it just sort of gave you a jolt when one skittered across.

Not only was Faye on the case, but Sawyer was also like Jorge's new right-hand man.

She didn't know how to thank her nephew, but she was going to figure that out.

He'd set up the four cabana units at Didi and Jorge's instruc-tion, and they were so cute! The yellow canvases had to be hosed off and the wooden lounges sanded here and there so no one got a splinter, but Sawyer took to the task like a champ. Jorge would mention where the sander was or how to adjust the mechanisms for the folding awnings and Sawyer would tinker with it until it was just right.

Ali would never have gotten to that before the guest arrivals.

Sawyer also decided pool care was his jam as well. He skimmed, added chlorine, and even scrubbed the sides while standing inside the pool. The kid was more into the cute tiles that lined the bottom and sides than any nineteen-year-old ought to be—but hey, there was no harm in that!

A last meeting with Silvio had the pool guy offering Sawyer a job if he decided to stay in Florida.

"Professional Pool Boy? No, you're not going to OSU for that," Faye had said to Sawyer when he enthusiastically told them about Silvio's offer.

Ali watched her sister crush her sweet nephew's hopes with one withering sentence. There was going to be a reckoning there, between them, Ali could see it, but in that moment at least, Sawyer shook off Faye's disapproval of working for Silvio. It was a nice offer, but in the end, Sawyer was only here for spring break. Still, Faye and Sawyer were on a collision course when it came to what they thought Sawyer's life should look like.

Sawyer finished getting the cabanas ready and then found other beach equipment he continued to dust off, oil up, and test out for the two families they had booked.

"I'll just be the beach guy this week, okay? I'll get them toys, set up the cabanas, clean the pool, do the beach towel wash, okay?"

Sawyer outlined his plan to Ali, and she was all for it.

"This week, we're here for your aunt," Faye reminded him. "If she's onboard, great, just don't get in the way."

"Get in the way?" Ali scoffed. "He's a godsend. You all are."

"Uh, keep in mind this kid asks me what the difference between bleach and detergent is every single time he gets near a Speed Queen," Faye said to Ali under her breath.

But for the most part, Faye let Ali and Jorge direct Sawyer, and he was smart enough to stay out of his mom's way.

Faye was just as task oriented as Ali. She'd spent a day setting up an irrigation system for the potted plans she was arranging around the pool. Rudy Palmer, their new frequent visitor, popped over every evening with suggestions. Faye and Rudy would sink deep into conversation over fertilizer, native plants, the effect of salt water, and on and on. Ali suspected the muscular Rudy Palmer was smitten with Faye. At the same time, Faye was smitten with learning about Zone 11b, from what Ali could see.

Ali decided Katie had worked plenty when it came to Ted and she insisted over and over that Katie didn't have to "work" while she was here.

But Katie, seeing Sawyer's industry, or maybe because she was Ali's daughter, also decided to pitch in.

"Look, manual labor, yeah, not a fan, but check this out!"

Katie had thrifted linens for the Mango Mansion and the Strawberry Hideaway. Ali had put all her efforts into those two cottages in preparation for their guests. And Katie had found table clothes, new throw blankets, and adorable pillows; just the right touches to make both cottages distinct, inviting, and comfortable after a day of sun and surf. They had gone from nice to—dare she say—stylish under Katie's meticulous eye for accessories.

"Katie, you have such a gift for the thrifted style," Ali complimented her daughter.

"Mom, you're the one who taught me how to thrift, duh. But I do like the two cottages. They look so good!"

Katie had moved from styling the little cottages to wandering around the inn. Ali had zero time to worry about the inn, and in her mind, it was a lower priority. She'd worry about getting full occupancy there next year after they proved what they could do for guests at the cottages. She hoped word would spread, and they'd book both! That was Ali's dream. To make it a reality, they had to do well with their first official guests, though. Ali was hoping her positive visualization and hard work would make her dream come true.

Ted was there, too, sort of pitching in. But somehow, everything he said gave Ali a little spike of panic, and he always keyed into something she hadn't thought of.

"I read that the lifeguard situation is a huge issue. They're hard to come by, and this pool is an attractive nuisance. But a nuisance, for sure. Maybe a sign to let people know they could die in the pool and you're not liable?"

That sent her into a low-grade panic. All that work on the pool, and what if someone drowned? OR what if the riptides got them at the beach?

Thankfully, Henry and Erica were there for her on that score.

The three of them had developed a ritual to have coffee on Wednesday morning at Erica's Morning Bell coffee shop. Having experienced small business owners as friends was a huge bonus.

"No, you don't need a lifeguard. Your pool already has signage. I'd also make sure there's no night swimming in the pool, but you can't tell the families not to swim in the ocean," Erica said, pointing out the obvious that, for some reason hadn't been obvious to Ali when she'd been talking with Ted.

"And the beaches are guarded. They drive up and down all day, you've seen them," Henry said.

"Right, I'm just getting cold feet," Ali confided to her friends.

"Look, we all do. My first week, remember, I was under water!

I mean, literally, the ice maker blew a gasket, and we had ankle-deep water in the kitchen, and then the inspector showed up and Erica here had to provide a distraction while I mopped up before he came back."

"Oh, man, yeah, I flirted my brains out and wound up stuck going to a movie with the inspector, all so he would get a good report that first week."

"Hey, you got a free movie out of it," Henry said.

"Uh, don't you remember, his credit card was declined, and I wound up paying? Needless to say, the relationship with the inspector did not turn into something bigger."

Ali laughed. The conversation had lightened her heart and her load.

Time with her new friends gave her the bandwidth to push on and do the final flurry of tasks to get ready for check-in day. Doubts and family minefields could wait.

It was almost time to show the world the new Sea Turtle Resort!

Twenty-One

BLAIR

She was at the bar of McGillivray's. Blake was out of town, and she just needed to have a drink or two before she went back to the apartment.

The apartment was no longer her sanctuary. When Blake first moved in, she thought it was cute that he wanted to make the space his.

This meant he wanted to stay. She didn't mind his framed poster of Indiana basketball. Or his gaming setup in the spare room. They were a team, and she'd happily make space for him. But that was before he became so bossy. Before he left his real job. Before he had a falling out with the partners for the social media marketing venture. Before she started drinking at the bar on a Wednesday night to get out of the apartment that was now more Blake with nothing of Blair. She and Darla, her sweet kitty, were being pushed to the margins of their own space.

Blair pulled out her phone. She opened her banking app.

She opened the account that Blake had no idea about. This was the secret account. This was her escape hatch.

It wasn't a lot. She'd managed to squirrel away ten thousand dollars. Over the last two years, Blake had taken her bigger nest egg and used it for his failed businesses.

When she realized, he would keep doing that, she started her secret fund. Was ten enough? She could buy a plane ticket and what? Start again somewhere?

She could tell her boss she was going to work remotely. She did online marketing. She could technically do that from anywhere.

But was ten enough? If she just waited a little longer, she could maybe pad that account a little more. But Blair was so tired of living with Blake.

She'd tried to get her mother's pearls out of hock, and as she'd suspected, they'd been sold within twenty-four hours. Blake didn't share the profits of that little theft. No. His money was his money, and her money was his money.

Blair also knew she'd been drinking too much. This was a Wednesday afternoon, and she just ordered her third drink. Or was it her fourth?

She' lost count.

And then she lost time. The last thing she remembered was being so sleepy.

And then a bright light was shining in her face.

Where am I?

She was dizzy. What was happening?

"Ma'am, get out of the car. Ma'am."

It was the police. Somehow, Blair had crashed her car. If they did a blood alcohol test on her, she'd be screwed.

She called Blake to get her a lawyer, to get her bail, to help however he could.

He didn't answer, but he was sure as heck there when she came home after the worst twenty-four hours of her life.

When Blake finished yelling at her for her stupidity and went in to start playing his video games, she went into their room and rolled her suitcase out.

She walked past him in the hallway, but his eyes were glued to the screens, and his earphones were on full blast. He had no idea she was leaving.

And that was just fine. Whatever love she had left for Blake disappeared long ago.

Twenty-Two

FAYE

Ali had done everything humanly possible to make The Sea Turtle Resort a great place for the two families they had booked.

Faye was worried that two was too small a sample to get the true measure of how Ali and her team would do handling full capacity, but based on the way the inn looked, it would be a while until they faced that situation.

Faye had cleaned the walkways and planted some flowers; she and Sawyer essentially picked up any slack they could. Ali continued to protest the help, insisting that Sawyer was supposed to be on spring break and Faye was allegedly retired.

They did manage to sneak in some beach time, and it was during that beach time that Faye had a moment to talk to her niece. Katie had pitched in by "styling" each of the spaces guests would have access to.

Faye didn't know what styling was. It sounded made up to her until she saw the before and after with Katie. She knew just the right vase to thrift, exactly where to put it in a room, and her touches helped make the renovations that Ali had done really sing.

Meanwhile, there had been an idea tickling the back of Faye's mind, and she decided to see if her niece would be game for it.

"Look, your mom is so busy with the cottages. I wonder if you and I could take a quick tour of the inn. See if there's anything we can leave your mom, like a to-do list or a vision board or something, for when she tackles the renovation there."

"How much work needs to be done there?"

"I don't know, but your eye is so good, I bet you can see if there's potential. Let's help your mom a little so she doesn't start from scratch."

"Okay, I'm game. Let's go now, though; I want to get good sun this afternoon."

Katie was still in the mode of getting sun. No matter how many times you told a twenty-something or teen that they'd regret sunburns, they gleefully ignored you. If Faye was honest, she sort of ignored it, too. She grew up working on her base and now she worked on making sure the sunscreen was a shield.

The great thing about Florida sun, though, was you didn't need much to feel like you were blooming. Before Katie hit the beach, she'd check out the inn and hopefully be inspired. Katie and Faye donned their beach coverups and flip-flops and went over.

"Okay, from the outside, I think you need to lean into this mid-mod thing. The cottages are very beach bum, almost lazy, but this inn is very...Astronaut's Wives Club. You know?"

"I think." Katie was right. There was a vibe here that said Mercury 7, 1960, pre-groovy but post-Eisenhower.

"I'd lean into bright yellow and orange, and whatever Mom has going with the cottages, do the opposite."

"You don't think they should be cohesive since it's one resort?"

"Do that with the outdoor furniture colors. Match the stuff you put outside there with the stuff that you do here."

"You're right."

"I'll sketch out what I'm talking about. Would that help?"

"Yes, and you're a genius, Katie Harris."

"I am, right?"

Faye put an arm around Katie. "You should have called me."

"What?"

"I heard you were underwater, dealing with your dad."

"Yeah, when Mom left, she left a mess."

Faye winced when she heard that. She didn't want to get in the middle of Ali and Katie's relationship, but she knew Ali hadn't told her daughter why she'd left Ted.

Faye didn't think Katie needed the details, but she did wish Ali would clue her in a little. Maybe then Katie would be less inclined to be Ted's doormat where Ali left off. Maybe then she'd give her mom a little break. Or not? The news that Ted was a much worse individual than Katie knew would not go down well. Faye chose to be very careful not to let on what she knew. She'd blurted enough when it came to Ted Harris. This was Ali's call, not Faye's.

"I'm your auntie. I live to make you happy. Call me next time."

"That's not what Sawyer says. I heard you two fighting the other day about college."

"Mom Faye is a real nag, but Aunt Faye, she's pure fun, I promise."

They toured the halls and peaked into the standard rooms. Faye put the focus back on the task at hand. That was better than telling her niece that her dad was a cad.

"Okay, now you say full atomic age for this place. You might be right. Check out the penthouse suite. Well, that's what Didi calls it, anyway."

It was going to be a lot of work; three times the work as the cottages. But Faye could see the only way they'd all get a good return on this place was full occupancy. The six cottages wouldn't be enough. They needed the hotel too and at this pace, it would be a long time before Ali could get to fixing up the inn for rental.

At the very least, she'd get a start on it, and with Katie's vision, she would have a plan of action. They walked through all the rooms and looked out the balconies, and Katie admired each little kitschy detail of The Sea Turtle Inn.

Faye could see her niece's wheels turning. *Success!* Katie was on board for Ali's dream, just like they all were. Katie promised to do some doodling.

"Okay, I release you. Sawyer was going to walk down to the Shell Shack. Maybe you can catch up with him there. For your consulting services." Faye handed Katie fifty dollars.

"Come on, you don't have to do that."

"Find Sawyer, and you two have lunch on me. You're both working hard on your vacation. You deserve to kick back."

"Sawyer is working hard. I'm just artfully dodging my parents while living off them. This is a full-time job."

"Girl."

Faye hugged Katie and watched the young woman skip off toward the beach. Damn that Ted, he really did just want to use her to take care of the things he didn't want to deal with—even if it stifled Katie's true potential. Just like he did with Ali.

She really hated her soon-to-be ex-brother-in-law.

Ali had closed the door on her marriage after the devastating realization about Ted's repeated betrayals. Yet, somehow, he was back, inching it open.

Faye was very suspicious of anything Ted did, and she was going to watch him closely. If he did anything else to undermine Ali's confidence in this project, she'd cold cock him.

Twenty-Three

ALI

Ali had about 500 places to be, which is, of course, why her car sputtered to its pathetic death.

Her 1999 Jeep Cherokee was a classic. That's what Ted called it, and she was happy to represent the brand linked with Toledo and get discounts thanks to Bruce's lifelong service to the company. They all drove Jeeps for pride and for the friends and family bennies.

Ali had been driving it for over twenty-five years. It was the car she had as a new wife and mom. Faye was into cars, obviously, and so was Bruce, and it was the one thing Bruce and Ted bonded over.

Ted loved his cars almost as much as he loved cheating on his wife, Ali thought, but then tried to squelch the bitterness when it intruded into her thoughts. All that was over. She had to move on.

Her preoccupation with, well, everything, had meant that she hadn't done a thing to maintain her old vehicle. That was actually one thing Ted always looked after.

As she was zooming down the highway doing the last round of

errands before they welcomed guests, about a million red lights blinked on along the dashboard.

Crap. Crap. Crap.

The power steering gave up the ghost, steam started rising from the front of the hood, and terror gripped her chest. She felt like the old *Six Million Dollar Man Show* opening line. *She's breaking up, she's breaking up!*

Ali was able to maneuver off the highway to the berm. She winced as traffic sped by her.

Ali never worried about oil changes or fluids or anything, and now, months past, when she'd driven this vehicle cross-country and pushed it to its limit doing errands for the business, the Jeep was pooped. Ali was on the side of Pinellas Highway, the car full of produce and food to supply the guests. She realized at that moment that she had also lapsed on her AAA coverage. If Ted did one thing right, it was car care. If Ali couldn't care less about something, it was car care.

And, of course, today was the day it decided to completely die. They were literally twenty-four hours away from check-in for the guests!

As the highway traffic screamed by, Ali realized she had no one to call.

Faye was two hours away, looking at some hotel she called "market research." Katie and Sawyer never answered texts or calls, plus they didn't have their own vehicles. She didn't want them to either, really; it would be dangerous, driving on the highway to fetch her. No, not them.

Ali wouldn't dream of calling Erica or Henry. They had already done so much for her, and she didn't want to be so darn needy! And the last thing she wanted was to get Didi or Jorge involved. She imagined them pulling up on the side of the highway with their truck. It was 100° in the shade, cars looked like they were speeding by her at 100 miles an hour, and the two of them were over 100 combined!

So, she did what came naturally. This was his area, after all. She called Ted.

Literally, within thirty seconds, he called back.

"Where are you?" he asked.

She gave him the location.

"Alright, make sure that you get away off the highway. People get killed all the time on the side of the road, either sitting in your car or, better yet, walking a few feet away."

That seemed a little excessive.

"I'm telling you: this is the highest risk you're going to have probably your entire life. I'm on the way."

She thought he was being dramatic, but the cars were going fast. She probably had more chance of facing an alligator on the side of the road than any other calamity. But one thing Ted was sure about was car emergencies. She decided she'd listen to her erstwhile nearly ex-husband one more time.

Ali had a car full of supplies, and she didn't want to lose those and the Jeep. She assessed her situation. No matter what happened, she was going to lose the perishable foods, but maybe she could save the dry goods she'd picked up.

Ali grabbed a few of the bags from the back and the passenger side and carefully got out of the Jeep. Man, it was hot.

As instructed, she walked ten feet away from the vehicle. The Florida sun that normally restored her and provided her midwestern Vitamin D depleted soul with light now felt aggressive and murderous when combined with traffic and no beach.

She stood there, waiting for Ted to arrive. He would know what to do. He probably already knew the best place to get a Jeep serviced in Haven Beach because, of course, he did.

Something felt familiar about this situation, even though it had never happened to her before. She couldn't put her finger on it. She realized she had a small smile on her lips, even in this predicament.

Ali stood there with her groceries, her bag, and her roll cart full of stuff that wouldn't spoil. In the distance, she thought she saw Ted's car. Her smile widened at the thought of eminent rescue.

Her phone buzzed, and she answered.

"Hey, I see you. I'm coming up behind you," Ted said.

She was relieved. As they ended the phone call, a car she wasn't paying attention to went slightly right of the yellow line in the right lane.

She yelled no, but it was like yelling in a dream. No one could hear her, and it felt like nothing really penetrated the thick air.

The car, a maroon sedan, hit her Jeep. It was a slow-motion scene, even though it all happened so quickly. The car hit the right side, where she would have been sitting. It rotated and skimmed farther off the highway. A fender went flying into the air, tires squealed, and bits of metal ricocheted in every direction.

Ali stood still, not knowing if any direction was safe.

The first move she made was with her head. She tracked the burgundy sedan. It was squealing now with the effort of the brakes.

It jerked to a stop. Time stood still for a moment.

Is everyone okay? What in the heck just happened?

And then the driver's side door opened fast, with no care to the danger of the traffic that was still whizzing by.

A man, who looked to be 100 or 120, got out. He wore polyester pants, light blue, and he had on a wide white belt to match white leather shoes.

He shook his head at her as if she'd done something wrong.

And then there was Ted.

"Oh my God, are you nuts? What the hell?" he yelled at the old man.

Ali didn't have words for what she had just seen. If she had been inside her car, she'd be—she didn't finish the thought to its deadly conclusion.

Ted turned his attention from the old man to Ali. He put his arms around her, and she finally snapped out of whatever shock she was in.

"Oh my God, thank God you weren't in the Jeep," he said.

He felt steady, strong, and familiar. Ali started shaking.

Ali realized the only reason she wasn't in the Jeep was because of Ted. He had told her to get out. He had told her to stand ten or more feet away. He had told her, and she had listened. And she was alive.

Twenty-Four

FAYE

When it came to Ali's near miss, all Faye could feel was relieved. While some would fret over what almost happened, Faye was the kind of person who focused on what did happen.

Her beloved big sister had walked away without a scratch even though her vehicle was totaled. Faye saw that as lucky, not unlucky.

She tried not to live in a space of doom. Sure, the first thought was her sister could have died, but her next thought was gratitude.

Faye also knew that the reason Faye moved from a place of "woe is me" to thankful was because of Ali. Her big sister always helped soften the blows of life and looked on the bright side. Even when they lost their mother so long ago, she could remember Ali's arm around her shoulders.

"Mommy would want you to keep planting flowers. She loved the flowers, and thanks to her, we always know she would love your flowers."

It was one of her earliest memories; she was sad about

Mommy, and then Ali showed her a way to see hope. Flowers kept her close with Mommy, all these years. Ali gave her that gift, not Mommy.

It was this mindset, passed down from Ali, that had allowed Faye to be grateful for a car accident. Ali had walked away from that crash. It could have been worse, but it wasn't.

But what middle child Faye had that Ali had less of was skepticism.

Ali's golden girl looks went hand in hand with her sunny perspective. Faye decided as a middle child she was more in tune with the brunette side of life.

She'd inherited a little more of the Bruce Kelly World View. While Ali was giving credit to Ted after the crash, Faye thanked fate and the Good Lord. Faye's gratefulness was also mixed with a major side-eye toward Ted. The incident had given Ted a new start in Ali's mind, and Ted was riding the wave of Ali's good graces.

Ted had warned Ali, and Ted had shown up when called, so now, Ted was forgiven? Not in Faye's book.

Faye could hold a grudge, and she had a big one against her soon-to-be ex-brother-in-law. What mystified her was that Ali didn't seem mad at Ted—the same Ted who was a cheater, the same Ted who wanted to take The Sea Turtle and cash it in as his own windfall. He'd brought lawyers in immediately to try to grab away half of Ali's dream. That was Ted.

Right now, though, Ted was "a lifesaver." Ali appeared to have issued him a free lifetime pass, a get-out-of-jail-free card, while Faye had begrudgingly granted Ted Harris a day pass, one free park admission. As far as Faye was concerned, he'd be back to the land of lousy soon-to-be ex-brother-in-law as soon as possible.

In the meantime, Faye tried not to fight with Ted. And she tried not to get in Ali's way. This was her marriage to end. Instead, Faye put her efforts into helping come up with a plan for the Inn at The Sea Turtle Resort.

Ali was focused on the two guests about to arrive and getting the two cottages ready. She'd restocked the supplies she'd lost in the crash.

Ted helped Ali find a new vehicle. Each day, Ted was helping Ali do this, or bringing up some issue that Ali "hadn't thought of."

Despite Faye's worries about Ted's comeback, Faye knew Ali better than she knew herself. Ali thrived with pressure like this, and she didn't need Faye underfoot as she got the cottages ready for their maiden voyage under Ali's management. She'd thought she'd spend time with her sister this week, but that meant Ted, too, all of a sudden. That was a recipe for disaster, so as a gift to Ali, Faye found a way to stay out of their orbit.

Faye had cleared the paths between the cottages and out to the beach. She'd added some potted flowers around the pool. And had a crash course in growing cycles beachside in Florida. She was in awe of what Rudy was doing at The Grotto. He had a ready answer for all her questions on growing, what she could clear, and what needed a permit.

But she was on hand when the guests arrived. Faye enjoyed watching Ali greet the families. Her Golden Dream Barbie of a sister really did shine when she was hosting.

Ali made each person checking in feel like they were now at their new beach home away from home, but she also added that touch of magic to let them know this was a special place.

The arrivals were staggered by four hours, and Ali gave both families a full welcome.

Meanwhile, the cottages themselves were so cute now!

Katie's touches had really turned each cottage into something that you'd see in a magazine! Curated Beachy Casual, was that a thing?

Didi and Jorge, along with Sawyer, handled the pool and the beach. The three of them had turned the pool from gunky to groovy

And Sawyer had really done a lot to fix up that beach area. He made sure the beach volleyball net he had installed was good to go.

He managed to make the cabanas look decent. Somehow, he'd found very cool pottery for her to plant her Grotto finds in the courtyard. He mentioned something about tiles or tile shopping or tile making. She tried not to meddle. She didn't want to fight with him the entire time they were here. Soon enough, this school thing would come to a head, and she'd have to be the bad cop again.

It was fun polishing the gem that was The Sea Turtle. And in between each project, Faye would take a moment and walk out to the ocean. She enjoyed early morning walks that stretched until the pier. She treated Sawyer to breakfast one morning at the Rods and Reels, a restaurant on the end of the pier that would cook up whatever fish you brought in. It was so fun, and it was so far from Ohio that it was easier to not think of her problems. She could put them on the back burner while they watched a pod of dolphins play just off the end of the dock. Miraculous!

In those moments, Faye unwound and just let time pass. Even ten minutes by the water felt like a spa treatment to her. She felt her jaw unclench, and her brow relax. What was it about the ocean?

More and more, Faye could see what The Sea Turtle must have looked like in its heyday, and it was another thing that kept her looking forward instead of inward. She did not want to look inward right now. Faye had too much of her own baggage to unpack, and she didn't want to. Retirement, Sawyer, finding a new job—it was all more than she wanted to deal with.

It was better for her rising anxiety to focus on something that was in worse shape than she felt she was, and that was The Sea Turtle Inn. By the time she and Sawyer headed back to Toledo, she'd have a good plan in place to maximize rental income at the resort and she'd have that kid of hers back in class.

Ali's vision was to give a four-star experience to her guests who were on reasonable budgets. She'd shared that vision with everyone at The Sea Turtle Resort. They'd all bought into what Ali wanted to do. And they were well on their way to achieving it with the inaugural guests.

The first night was lovely. The Grand Finale was such an amazing tradition. Everyone's troubles seemed to melt for an hour or so while the sun set over the water. They said no two Ohio snowflakes were the same, and Faye had learned that no two Florida sunsets were either. The colors were always different, sometimes subtly so, but other times it was like a different planet!

Faye had also gotten used to seeing Henry at the Grand Finale, but for some reason, Henry was now AWOL.

It couldn't hurt to ask Ali. Heck, it would do Ted some good to see Henry around. She missed Henry and the effect he had on Ali. *More Ted and less Henry going in the wrong man direction*, Faye thought.

Faye approached Ali with her little pot-stirring question. Ali and Faye were both in gorgeous retro Kaftans provided by Didi's excellent vintage supply. They were the perfect outfit for sunset and wine.

"Hey, where's Henry?" she asked.

"Oh," Ali said, "he decided to give Ted, Katie, and me space. It's nice. I mean, he's been through a divorce; he knows it can be awkward, so he's staying over at The Seashell Shack these days."

Faye wanted to say if he's just a friend, why would showing up be an issue? She didn't say anything, but she did give Ali a look. Ali knew exactly what Faye was thinking.

"Henry and I are just friends. What?" Ali jutted her jaw at Faye. This was her pointed but silent way to tell her to butt out. Faye shrugged and Ali flitted over to the guests to be sure they had all they needed.

So much the better. Faye wanted to sound off about Ted but now wasn't the time.

The good news? Erica had shown up with cookies for the kids and breakfast to set out for the guests for the next morning. She was loaded down with delicious food. Erica had wanted to give the food to Ali for free, as a friendship thing, and Ali insisted on paying. This was a business, Ali said, and Erica's Morning Bell was a business. Another legacy of Bruce Kelly: no free rides. Pay your way. As Erica came in laden with goodies, Ted swooped in and, shocker, volunteered to help.

"Here, let me." Ted had offered to take the food in. Ted was trying to be useful. But Faye thought she knew why.

Erica found Faye after she'd said her hellos. Erica was one of those people that cut right to the heart of the matter. It made Faye glad Ali had Erica's good sense when Faye wasn't in town.

And at the heart of the matter with Ali right now was a resurgence of her formally DOA marriage.

"Wow, so was Ted less of a knob when they dated or something?" Erica remarked, handing Faye a glass of wine. Faye tried not to laugh too loud at Erica's assessment.

"He was smart, charming—he used to look like Tom Cruise. Pre-couch jumping Tom Cruise. Ted seemed worldly. That was really it. He seemed smart and worldly. We weren't that. Ali wanted to know more about the world but didn't have the resources to move far away from home to learn it. I guess that was the idea with Ted. He was more Toledo, Spain than Toledo, Ohio. On paper, anyway, and a long time ago."

Faye thought back to what Ted was like when Ali first started dating him. They were a blue-collar family, and Ted offered a high-brow sensibility. Of course, it was all b.s.

"Look, I've got no room to judge. I made a huge mistake in my twenties, a real dud first marriage. I wouldn't want anyone to think I was the type of person who would marry the man I married, but I did."

"Same, Sawyer's dad, Bud, was worse than a dud."

"Got it. Well, here's to having the maturity to avoid the duds and Buds."

"And not backsliding," Faye said, and they both looked at Ali, who was laughing at something Ted had said.

"Yeah, here's to not backsliding." Faye and Erica clinked wine glasses.

And they watched the sunset. Today's sunset was purple, orange, and pink. Faye knew it was the same sun that set over her house and her little garden back home, but somehow it was more vibrant here. Somehow, having the blue ocean and the purple sky meet on the horizon did things to the water and air that couldn't be imagined in her little Ohio home.

The guests of The Sea Turtle Resort and Cottages clapped as the big orange orb sank into the ocean. Ali was beaming. This was what Ali was after—giving this experience to her guests. Faye was proud of Sawyer, Ali, Katie, and even a little of herself. They'd pulled it off!

She slept a little easier that night, knowing that the guests were here, that Ali had it under control, and that maybe this business idea would work.

It would all work out. That thought along with the wine from the Grand Finale lulled her into a peaceful sleep that night.

Her peaceful slumber with a side of ocean breeze ended abruptly the next morning, when a series of crises unfolded.

Faye heard legitimate yelling.

She pulled on her cutoff shorts, her Detroit Tigers t-shirt, and a pair of flip-flops and hustled out the door. The brief realization crossed her mind that at home, she'd still be donning layers to withstand the windchill, even for a quick run to her mailbox at the end of the driveway.

Faye moved in the direction of the commotion. She walked from the inn to the courtyard in the center of the cottages to investigate.

There, she found the Dean Family squaring off against Ali!

Ali was apologizing over and over again.

"I am so sorry, of course! Of course!"

The family was literally putting their stuff in their mini-van at a breakneck pace.

Are they checking out? Already?

Their minds were made before Faye had even put on her flip-flops.

Sawyer was there, hauling suitcases and toys and whatever else Sheri Dean ordered him to do. And Ali wasn't arguing with the guests; she was actually helping them leave instead of reminding them they'd lose their deposit.

"And I expect a full refund, FULL, or you're going to be hearing from my lawyer."

Faye could not imagine what had been so egregious.

Katie was also there to witness the scene. She stood back from the fray with Faye.

"Do you know what they're talking about?" Faye asked under her breath.

"Yeah, so they were eating breakfast that had been delivered to the table on the porch, and they opened up the wrapping, and I guess a bunch of bugs were in there, like spiders or something."

"Oh, my gosh, how in the world?"

Katie shrugged and all Faye could do was watch Ali try to get the Dean Family out of the resort so that the Bowman Family didn't get wind of the calamity.

Faye saw now that containing the damage was Ali's plan. Ali would hustle out the Deans in hopes it was an anomaly.

Spiders in the food? Faye gave an involuntary shudder.

So much for the lovely inaugural weekend of the new-and-improved Sea Turtle.

Her phone buzzed. It was Rudy. She decided to take the man up on an offer he'd made her. Getting out of the way seemed like a good play right about now. Ted was playing the big man and if Faye didn't get out of there, she was going to say something she shouldn't, again.

"I changed my mind, that offer you made for the tour? I'm in."

"Great, pick you up tomorrow morning."

Twenty-Five

BELINDA (DIDI) 1985

The wedding was beautiful, the honeymoon a dream. Joetta and Banks had gone to St. Thomas for a week. And now they were back. Joetta and Belinda were eating lunch at The Armstrong Country Club; Joetta was now the First Lady of the place that Belinda merely managed.

But the specter of her nieces that wasn't so easy to dream away.

The girls and what would happen to them weighed on her mind day-in and day-out.

They picked at cucumber sandwiches, and Belinda dutifully looked at the pictures Joetta handed her one by one.

Belinda felt like she was in some Edgar Allen Poe story, the Tell-Tale Aunt. Her heartbeats were shadowed by the three little girls in Toledo, weren't Joetta's?

Finally, she put down her fancy teacup and laid her cards on the table.

"Look, Joetta. We have to talk about it."

"Talk about what?"

Joetta was as healthy and bright-eyed as she looked the day she left Florida over a decade ago now. She'd been going to her AA meetings. She was in love. She was rich again. Joetta was the beautiful, adoring, and adored wife of the right kind of husband this time. It clearly made all the difference.

Still, how could Joetta move on? How could she?

Here it goes, Belinda thought, *time to burst Joetta's bubble*.

"I think you need to go back to Toledo because he's been able to...He's been able to hang up on me. He won't even answer if he thinks it's from you, but I think if he sees you and sees that you really are a different person, that you've really stopped drinking, he might change his mind. You could bring the girls here."

Upon Belinda's mention of the girls, Joetta went from wide-eyed bride to something else entirely. She became stiff from her shoulders to her hands. She dropped her teaspoon on the table, and she narrowed her eyes at her big sister. This was not an expression Joetta had ever had; it was altogether formidable.

"I'm going to show you something."

She pulled out of her pocket a letter. "I have 15 of these letters. I wrote three every day once I started back at AA, even just to get him to listen to an apology. They're all returned to sender, but it's worse than that."

She pulled out another piece of paper. There it was—a copy of the arrest report, a copy of her mugshot, and a picture of the car. When Belinda saw the photo of the car, she realized what was really motivating Bruce Kelly. The girls could've died. They were lucky. Seeing it versus hearing about it was a different story.

"If Mom and Dad see this, I'm out. I will have nothing from them. I just now got back in their good graces. And I must be married now. Do you understand?" Joetta put her hands over her middle. Her sister was finally ready to talk about the real issue. She may like Banks Armstrong, but she loved what he could provide in the face of a familiar situation for Joetta. Pregnancy.

"Who's?" That was a question that Belinda had wanted to ask

from the moment she realized Joetta was pregnant again. Belinda also knew the answer.

"I'm more pregnant than I should be. But I'll deal with that later. I was underweight, that helped."

"What about the plan to give them The Sea Turtle?"

"I signed it over. It's in the girls' names. He won't answer me. Sent a legal letter, too."

Belinda swallowed; she had tried just as hard. Bruce Kelly wouldn't budge.

"I would move back to Toledo and live in the basement or an apartment or on the damn street if I could be with my girls. But he is out to destroy me. Bruce won't let me be a part of their lives. And I have accepted that he is right. And I was a danger to them. I suppose I could live on the street, but --" Joetta looked down at her own middle. Her sister was protecting a new child, and was trusting that Bruce would protect the girls.

Belinda teared up and then blinked. A deep well of strength seemed to be rising from her once flighty little sister.

"We did what we could. Here's how this is going to go. We keep the manager of The Sea Turtle. We direct him anonymously. I've set up a bank account for the operations and the surpluses will go to the girls. At least they'll have that."

Joetta had taken care of legal and financial arrangements. This was a new Joetta, for sure. The old Joetta had zero ability to do anything practical. This was a Joetta with an edge that was sharpened. Belinda was both impressed and scared. Life had made Joetta a different woman.

Again, tears pooled in Joetta's eyes. She loved her girls. She wanted to be their mother. But maybe that was the ultimate expression of selflessness. Letting them go. Her sobriety was a new thing, tenuous. What if she fell off the wagon? It was a risk Bruce saw and it might be fueling Joetta too.

Belinda slid a tissue to Joetta. "Here, your mascara is going to run. That won't do."

"I'm doing all I can. I am going to keep working on the AA program. I don't want to mess it up. If there's one thing I know, I was a bad mom. And I can't be that again."

"No, you weren't. You made a beautiful home in Toledo for those girls."

"Well, when I was sober. What if going back to Toledo meant I also went back to my old habits? I need to try to start fresh. As fresh as I can."

Belinda reached out her hand and put it over Joetta's. "It's okay. I'll manage the manager of The Sea Turtle, and I'll keep an eye on the girls, you know, from afar. They'll have a good life, and you will too. And maybe, after time passes...?"

"I can't talk about them anymore. I can't even think about them. It's too hard."

It was an impossible situation. It felt like everyone involved was doing what they thought was best for Ali, Faye, and Baby Blair, but nothing was right. This couldn't be right.

But after a lifetime of Belinda taking the lead and Joetta impulsively following her fancy, Joetta was the one in charge. She was steely in her determination.

And the plan was set. The Sea Turtle profits would go to the girls, Belinda would keep her mouth shut, and Joetta would start over and try like heck to do it right this time.

Twenty-Six

FAYE

Rudy told her to wear clothes she didn't mind getting wet or dirty. In fact, he said it's always good to have a bathing suit. It is Florida, after all. So, with her sister regressing into her old marriage and her son doing whatever Jorge needed, Faye decided it wasn't selfish to escape for a little bit with the handsome guy who loved plants as much as she did.

Rudy picked her up shortly after the sun came up. She knew her sister was up, so she popped into the office. "Hey, Ali, I'm going to be gone for a few hours."

"Oh yeah? A hot date with a local surfing instructor?"

"No, I don't have a hot date, but I do have an excursion. Let's just call it that."

"Oh really? Who are you going on an excursion with?"

"Rudy Palmer and I are going to, I guess, look at plants."

"Is that what the kids call it today? Looking at plants? Don't let him give you a hickey. Dad will ground you," Ali said.

Faye figured it was her turn to get the ribbing. She'd been

ripping on Ali about Henry every chance she got. She'd take a little teasing if it meant it kept the conversation away from Ted.

"Alright, alright," Ali tossed a white tube towards Faye, who caught it.

"Sunscreen," Ali said.

"See you in a bit."

"Take your time. This was supposed to be a vacation, and you've worked the entire time."

Faye brushed off her sister's admonition and walked out to the front of The Sea Turtle into the parking lot. Rudy Palmer was leaning on the Mangrove Garden Grotto pickup truck, ready to go. It was 7 AM on the dot.

He looked her up and down. "You got a bathing suit?"

"Yes, I have a bathing suit."

"Under all that?" He pointed to her t-shirt and shorts. All that wasn't that much if you compared it to the multiple layers she'd be wearing at home.

"Yes, if you must know."

"Alright, let's hit it."

They drove for about 10 minutes in and around Haven Beach. Haven Beach was just a small section, not much more than five miles along the Gulf, but there were little streets that she hadn't seen, alcoves that she would never have explored had she not been with someone who knew the terrain. Faye didn't know what "Old Florida" was, though she heard people lament that it didn't exist anymore. If it did, it was here. The funky little lanes that dissolved into sand that led to the beaches and the hold-out old houses next to the condos. Those were the remnants of Old Florida she suspected.

After their quick drive, he parked the truck and got out to pull two surfboards from the back.

"Listen, I don't know how to surf," she said.

He laughed. "No, there's not really good surfing here. We don't have the high enough waves. These are standup paddleboards or SUPs."

She'd heard of something like that before but had never tried it. "I mean, I'm in shape, dude, but whatever this is, I've never done it."

"This is the easiest, most relaxing, and quietest way to see some of the vegetation along the south side of Haven Beach. Come on, you're super fit, and you'll be able to pick it up fast," he said. She was happier than she should have been at his compliment about her fitness. Hard work and an estrogen patch were her secret weapons.

"It's a big surface, and you'll balance easily. Just start with a wide stance. Turn with the paddle on the front of the board and sweep to the back. Reverse that to change directions." She was nervous, but she knew how to swim, and he'd made her wear a life jacket. The water was calm. She wondered about alligators but decided not to ask. Faye set her mind and disconnected her old lady worries and just go for it. She was going to add supping to her list of adventures.

Rudy got in the water, and she followed. She was sitting at first.

"Now, here's how you stand up," he said, showing her how to post one leg and then the other. She did the same. At first, she felt a little unstable. Rudy was right, though. It was big enough to make her feel stable fairly quickly.

"I gave you the biggest board. It's going to stay under you, and it's going to be the easiest way to get close to some of these mangrove tunnels. I mean, it is the name of our county."

It didn't take long for her to get the hang of it. Rudy told her that if she got tired, she could just sit.

"You can always sit on the paddleboard. There is no shame in it. Just follow me over there. Leave that shark alone, and it won't bother you."

"What!"

"Just kidding, it's a dolphin."

"Look, if you see a shark, I expect you not to tell me. I do not want to see a shark. Do you understand me?"

He laughed.

"Got it. Dolphins only."

She kept an eye on Rudy but soon got more and more confident.

"I don't want to get swept out to sea."

"Don't worry, we're going to hug the coastline. I won't get you near any big currents."

Why did she trust Rudy? Faye couldn't put her finger on it, but she did feel like a good judge of character. She was duped once by her husband, but mostly, she read people right. Rudy was good-natured, strong, funny, and loved plants. *Anyone who loved plants had to be a good person, right?*

With Rudy in the lead, she dipped her paddle down into the water and across the board. She would switch sides if she saw herself going too far in one direction or another, but eventually, he said, "Here. This is what I meant. It's best to sit."

Rudy sat on his paddleboard, and she did the same. She watched how he navigated while sitting, and they moved their way into a little inlet.

"Duck your head," he instructed. The paddle boards were more like kayaks now, and even sitting, she had to hunch down a little.

"What is all this?"

"It's a mangrove tunnel."

Faye couldn't believe her eyes. It was like an entirely different world, or planet even. The roots of the mangrove were like hundreds of ropey strands stretching into the water. They twisted around each other, entwined into the water and up. Stretching over them were the waxy mangrove leaves everywhere she looked. It was a canopy of foliage and a symphony of natural sounds.

Faye followed Rudy but then soon forgot about everything

else. Her paddle swished into the water, and her eyes were wide at each new turn. It was cooler here than in the open water.

"How do you feel about stingrays?"

"I feel fine about them."

"Oh good, there's a stingray." Rudy nodded toward the left of his board, and they both stopped paddling for a moment and watched the stingray. It seemed to fly underwater.

For three hours, Faye was immersed in this new world. They only paddled back because she was starting to feel like she didn't have much left in the tank. She wanted to stay all day, but her ankles were trembling with the effort to stay balanced. Rudy kindly noticed and let Faye know that he was getting a little tired, too. He probably wasn't, but he was sweet to a newbie standup paddle boarder.

He loaded their boards into his truck and Faye didn't say much. She was trying to recall all the sensations, the sights, and the sounds of the mangrove tunnel.

"Well, what did you think," Rudy asked as they drove back to the Sea Turtle.

"I think that was the best not date I've ever had in my entire life," Faye replied.

"Dang, I knew I should have gone in for a kiss back there."

She smiled at him and was grateful he hadn't. The day had been perfect, just the way it was.

Twenty-Seven

ALI

Ali tried to regroup. Even while accommodating the furious Deans, she had asked Didi and Jorge to be sure to grab the food so they could inspect it.

If there were spiders in the cottage or an infestation of some sort, she needed an exterminator. Jorge had sealed a croissant in a Tupperware container with a few of the spiders.

It gave her the total ick, but she needed to know if this was a fluke or a full-on insect invasion.

The idea of liability that Ted had planted in her mind emerged front and center.

What if these were dangerous spiders? What if one of the Dean kids were allergic to spiders? Or gluten or seawater?

Lawsuits were scarier than sharks, she decided.

The food had been sealed in plastic. Erica had delivered it immaculately as usual and placed it on the porch of the cottage. However the spiders got in there, it was ultimately Ali's mistake. The buck stopped with her on all things. That was the way she ran the Frogtown and the way she was going to run The Sea Turtle.

Didi tried to reassure her. "Oh honey, it's OK. They're not the only game in town. There are other guests, other fish to fry!"

It was that attitude that had led to the state of The Sea Turtle before Ali had arrived. Didi wasn't exactly complacent, but maybe, at her age, she just didn't have the drive like Ali had. Four-star hotels weren't run by women in kaftans, were they?

Ali knew the clock was ticking loudly on this endeavor. And every guest who walked away unhappy meant the potential that a hundred more would read a scathing Yelp review. Still, she had to keep her focus on the remaining guests.

Ali poured her efforts into that.

Mid-morning, Erica called, sounding a little panicked. "Honey, I heard about the food situation. I guarantee you it was perfectly good when I brought it last night!"

"Oh, it didn't even cross my mind that you had anything to do with it. I think I just...I have an infestation or something."

"I feel terrible. I did a kitchen search here and in my car and..."

"I'm serious. This was on my end. This place isn't up to speed yet. That's really it."

"Well. if I'm still invited, I'll see you tonight for the Grand Finale. I think a glass of wine is definitely in order."

"Invited? You're family now. I'd be offended if you missed it! And thanks for calling. Don't worry, I'm okay, it's okay," Ali reassured her.

Ali was being truthful. She didn't think of Erica's food in any way as the problem. Ali had seen it for herself—it was fine. What she had to do now was push forward and make sure it didn't happen again.

The Bowman family was spending the day at Busch Gardens. Busch Gardens wasn't exactly Disney, but it wasn't chopped liver. It was a fun theme park— a little bit more affordable—and the kids would be tuckered out by the end of the day. Kids sleeping after a fun day, with a sea breeze wafting through their charming beachfront rental, would be a lasting memory for the family. She knew it. It would be fine. More than fine.

With only one family to care for, nothing would get in the way of Ali giving them that four-star service.

The Grand Finale was one thing, but she took care to think about what they'd want after spending a day on their feet. She made sure their beds were in, made the towels fresh—and Ted even helped!

He'd replaced a flickering bathroom light that would have driven anyone nuts if it was on at night.

There was spider-free food, ready to go for the Grand Finale, there were cold beverages, and it was all set.

The Dean Family Disaster would be a blip, a thing of the past, a learning experience, Ali told herself over and over.

She figured the Bowmans would be back around dinner or after. Ali spent the rest of her time with the million other tasks that seemed to always be popping up at The Sea Turtle.

Katie stopped her as she was sweeping off the walkway in the courtyard. She was wearing the shortest shorts one could imagine and a tank top. Her girl was so beautiful. The mass of blonde hair piled on top of her head indicated the signs of a functioning thyroid and hormones that worked for her, instead of—as Ali knew in her forties—against her. *Alas...*

Katie greeted Ali with an unexpected embrace. Ali got a whiff of the coco butter Katie slathered on after a day in the sun. How sweet she was finally turning out to be. The teenage Katie doled out affection merely to get the car or money to spend at the Franklin Park Mall. The now twenty-year-old Katie was coming out the other side. Ali could see glimpses of the sweet little girl and the mature adult all rolled into the package that was her daughter.

"Mom, those people this morning were just jerks. They totally overreacted to such a little thing."

"No, honey, it wasn't just a little thing. You'd freak out if that was your food," Ali said.

"Yeah, probably."

Maybe someday Katie would inherit this place! If she did, she'd need to understand how to see to the details. Ali tried to put a swift end her own wild dreaming.

Inherit? They may not get through the first week!

"Hey, did you see the drawings I did for Aunt Faye?"

"No, gosh, I would love to see them. Show me!"

She didn't really have time to spend with Katie and the drawings, but Katie had an eye and a flair. And Ali needed some good news. It was very optimistic to think they'd survive this week and get to fixing up the Inn, but Ali wanted to think positively. She had to.

Katie opened her laptop and pulled up one image after another of the busted-looking Sea Turtle.

"Ugh, yeah, there's so much to do over there." This fun moment with Katie was getting a little depressing.

Katie clicked her mouse, and the same photos transformed each space into a groovy-looking, mid-century modern dayglo paradise.

Ali could almost imagine what it was like in the fifties. If it looked like this, of course Frank Sinatra would come to stay!

"Oh my gosh, these are so cool!" Ali said.

"Thanks, Mom. My design instructor always says I should lean into whatever the environment tells me to do. This was it. I mean, I watched *The Right Stuff* and a couple of *Mad Men* episodes to come up with some of this, but not bad, right?"

"Not bad at all!"

Katie's renderings had achieved the effect Ali had hoped for. Ali didn't even know that's what she wanted at the Inn until Katie coaxed it out. Ali was bolstered and encouraged. They really had the raw materials here for something spectacular.

Still...this all looked like an expensive renovation. Katie had an amazing vision, and a funky style all her own. But what she didn't have was the reality of a budget. That would be Ali's department. Ali wondered if she could find some of these things Katie had pictured in area consignment shops.

She flipped through the images, and it gave her hope for what could be for The Sea Turtle. She also felt grateful for Faye. Faye was the one who'd turned her attention to the Inn while Ali was dealing with the cottages. It was Faye who had enlisted Katie to come up with a plan. They'd filled in the gaps that Ali needed. That was what family was supposed to do, and Ali felt hers had come through in a million ways this week.

Ali told Katie how proud she was of her.

"Thanks, Mom. I'm very much in need of a shower."

Katie headed to the cottage, and Ali knew it was getting close to the time for the Bowmans to get back.

Busch Gardens wasn't open late today, so Ali decided to check in on them. She wanted to make sure they knew they had complimentary food for tonight's Grand Finale by the beach. Nothing better after a day of walking on the hot cement of a theme park than sinking your feet into the sand.

She saw their cottage door was open, and there was a flurry of activity. They were back!

Ali walked toward the cottage, and the momentary feeling of hope sank into her stomach like a stone. It was déjà vu all over again. Something was decidedly very wrong.

"This is disgusting. We can't stay here, Mom!" one of the kids said. The family was in an uproar. It was the same scene as before, with a different issue.

"What's wrong? What can I do?" Ali asked.

She had just been in the cottage a few hours before. What could possibly have happened?

"The toilet is completely overflowing. It's all over the floor," said Carrie Bowman.

Her sister, Betty Bowman, agreed and egged her on. "We are *not* paying for this," Betty said.

Betty, as far as Ali knew wasn't paying for any of it, but okay. Ali went into damage control mode.

"Oh, my goodness, please, please let me help. We can move all your stuff out of the area, and I can—"

"Darn right, we're moving our stuff. We're moving our stuff out of here and into the Courtyard Inn," Carrie said.

"Oh, goodness, I'm sure I can fix this. I can move you right into another cottage." She'd cleaned out the Dean's cottage. That could work. It was even a little bigger.

"Oh, where the infestation is?"

Ugh. Word of the spider invasion had spread to the Bowmans. Spiders and now sewage. Some four-star hotel this was! All of Ali's dreams of an ocean-side paradise were turning into nightmares.

"The Courtyard pool has a pirate slide," Ali heard one of the Bowman kids say.

"I'm sorry, lady," said the dad, Kevin, who was now pointing his finger in her face. "What kind of organization are you running? I have half a mind to sue you for contaminating us."

It was a toilet overflow, not Chernobyl. What the heck?

At that point, Ted showed up out of nowhere.

"What's the problem here, sir?" Ted said, standing between Ali and Kevin. "I'm sure—"

"—The problem is raw sewage in the middle of the floor! You got a problem with me telling the manager this place is a rip-off?"

"No, I don't have a problem with that. I have a problem with your tone," Ted said.

The people Ali had been trying to give the most peaceful and wonderful experience were about to get into a fistfight with Ted. Carrie and Kevin Bowman were going to hit something if this kept getting hotter. And Ted was a hot head.

"Ted, please, it's okay. I just want to make this right," Ali said. She had her most apologetic, non-confrontational voice going.

The voice that calmed down irate union bosses and self-important air-conditioning business owners.

Ted did not want to de-escalate. He didn't know the meaning of the word.

"I suggest you leave now," Ted said. He stood in between Ali and the entire Bowman family as though this was about to be an actual war.

What did he just say?

Ali tried to back the train up, but it was too late.

"You don't have to say it twice, buddy," Kevin said.

"Wait, no!"

"Let him go, Ali. You don't need their business," Ted said.

Wrong. Ali needed all the business she could get, but it was too late. These guests, like the earlier guests, were disgusted with her.

Ali heard the family talking as they packed their stuff. "So glad we got that call from that hotel. The fact that they have rooms left it's a miracle," said Betty Bowman.

They were ready to go in less than ten minutes. Ali could only watch.

Tears welled up in her eyes as they drove away.

The cottage was now empty. The inn was empty.

Ted looked sympathetic.

"I told you; this is not what you think it is. This is a much more difficult job than just putting cute towels out."

For the first time since she moved to Florida, Ali felt like Ted might be right. She also felt like Ted was the only one who understood how much pressure she was under.

Twenty-Eight

FAYE

Faye knew their vacation was coming to a close, so she'd been on the beach, walking, enjoying the view, and generally trying to figure out what to do with her life.

When she started to feel slightly crispy from the sun, it was time to head back to the inn. She entered on the far side of the hotel building, bypassing the cottages. Best to stay far away from Ted if she didn't want to spoil her day of sun and relaxation.

The inn was empty and quiet, and she headed up to the penthouse suite for a nice relaxing shower.

When she got to the room, she heard a buzzing. And there, on the table in the corner, was Sawyer's phone. Faye's darker instincts took over.

There were two schools of thought when it came to cell phone usage and today's kids. One school believed parents should be very hands-off. Parents in this school respected their children's privacy.

And then there was Faye.

She'd pushed Sawyer to play outside and not always on

screens. Faye had always been very careful and strict when it came to cell phones and social media. Sawyer had just got on social media this year, well, with his own accounts. She knew he scrolled and chatted on his gaming systems. But still, she did not allow her kid to "go play on the phone," and she wasn't going to let him text his junk to some girl. Nope. She was on it. And Sawyer knew it.

Now, to be fair, she had removed the family tracking app after Sawyer had moved to college. She didn't want to know when he was out at the bar or wherever. She wanted him to be out at the bar or wherever. It was Ohio State. Of course he was!

It had been over a year since she'd tracked him on his phone or spied on his texts when he wasn't looking. Faye had adjusted to giving up control and oversight of Sawyer's phone.

But now it was vibrating. He was getting a message.

Faye didn't want to do it. But he'd left it on the dresser in the sitting area of their suite.

She would just take a little peek.

Faye read the bubble. He had a new email.

Who was emailing him? Kids don't email. Right?

Faye stopped debating herself. Her son was floundering, and she was still paying the bills. A little invasion of privacy was in order one last time. Maybe if she wasn't a single parent, she'd have someone to bounce this off, but it was all her.

She wanted it that way, but that also meant if Sawyer was making bad decisions, she'd be the one to clean up the mess and get him on the right track. With her justifications in place, she typed in the password of the lock screen.

Faye knew Sawyer's password because it was always *DavidLee-Roth84*—for some reason, the kid loved David Lee Roth circa 1984.

She wasn't a helicopter mom, usually. But Sawyer had been telling her he was taking care of his next semester. She had to check, and then she'd leave him alone. She'd just take a quick look.

And sure enough, the email was from osu.edu. It was an admissions office email, and she just had to see it.

She quickly scanned the email, and there it was in digital black and white: proof that he had dropped out of Ohio State. Her mind raced.

Words like "deadline" and "re-enrollment requirements" caused her to feel nauseous.

Was there a way to undo it? Was there a way to fix this? Could he still get his classes for next semester? Could they get him in at the last minute? Certainly, his grades weren't that bad. He wasn't suspended from school. He was willingly dropping out. He hadn't failed everything. He didn't have great grades, but he hadn't failed.

At the root of her reaction was the undeniable belief that she had failed as a mom. She wasn't going to get this kid over the finish line.

Faye stood there looking at the email from the admissions office. How could she undo the damage he'd done by missing the deadlines and dropping out? Her mind was cycling through options, phone in hand.

That's when Sawyer walked in.

Crap. Busted.

"What are you doing?"

No use in denying it. She was here to fix this mess not make friends with her son.

"I'm reading an email."

"Okay, but that's my phone."

"Excuse me? The phone I pay for?" Never a great way to engender trust, but there it was. She was having a full-parent meltdown.

"Mom, that's a violation of privacy!"

"Sawyer, what is this?" she demanded. "You said you were going to get it together and finish out the year at least."

She'd had this argument with him nearly every day since he started at OSU. He had every opportunity in the world. She'd

worked herself to the bone, making sure to give him those oppor-
tunities, and here he was, throwing it all away.

"Mom, I don't like it. I don't want to stay there. I don't want
to go into accounting. I don't want to go into advertising or pack-
aging or communications. None of it."

OSU had every possible major. That was one of the reasons
they'd picked it. Sawyer was undecided, but he could decide there.
They'd help him decide. He could be nearly anything at that giant
school. The options were unlimited.

But if he just quit...

"But Sawyer, you're only nineteen."

She didn't know what else to say. She'd made all the other arguments since before he even started high school. Keep your options
open by getting good grades, by being good at sports, by getting a
degree. She felt he was willingly closing doors to his own future.

She had made every threat. She had made every deal. She had
made everything easy. Maybe that was the problem. It was too easy
for Sawyer to just throw away his future.

"What do you expect to do if you do not go to school?"

Sawyer didn't say anything. Usually quick with the retort or
even the lie that reassured her, Sawyer was quiet now in the face of
her, asking the same question she'd always asked.

*What are you going to do when you grow up? When are you
going to grow up?*

"Mom, I want to stay here."

This was not the answer she wanted nor expected in the least.

"Florida? Florida is a vacation, not a life."

"Not according to Aunt Ali, or Miss Didi, or Mr. Jorge."

She'd encouraged her sister to live out her dream here, to go for
it. But this was different. This was her son. How could he even
know what was available anywhere, much less here, if he dropped
out of school? This was a second act for Ali, not where you started.

Who started here? Mickey Mouse?

"What are you going to do here?" She was incredulous. She

plowed ahead, her thoughts and doubts tumbling out of her mouth. "We're helping your aunt. We're not working at the hotel. We're not going to cut into the revenue this place might or might not earn by asking your aunt to put us on the payroll. This whole thing could crash around her ears, and I don't want it to. I want it to succeed wildly, amazingly, but that's her dream, not yours."

"I'm not asking for any handouts," Sawyer said. "I mean, it'd be nice if I could stay somewhere on the property while they fix up the inn, but even so, I've got a line on a job."

It was like he was speaking a different language. Everything her kid said was a new thing, something she didn't expect or plan for.

Did he say "job"? "A line on a job"?

"You've got a line on a job?"

Was this the pool boy thing? She'd spoiled him, that was it. He had no idea how hard the world could be.

She took a breath. Okay, a job. She tried to find the ray of light in the situation. At least he knew he had to work. She thought about his dad. That was something his dad missed completely— heading to work. She tried not to think about Sawyer's dad. She knew why. She knew her deepest fears for Sawyer lay in that line of thinking. Instead, her own dad raised his voice in her subconscious: honest work. Was it honest work?

"What is this job? Is it honest work?" she asked, her voice tight.

"It's an apprenticeship, yes, I think that's honest work. I mean, what the heck is honest work?"

It was a phrase from another time, Faye realized.

Faye was angry. She was scared. She was frustrated. All of the work that she had put into Sawyer, into making sure he took the right classes, into making sure he went to the right camps for soccer, into making sure they had his transcripts for school, into finding sheets to fit the XL twin beds at Ohio State—*all of it*—the waste!

Nineteen was a dangerous age. Some decisions you made casually at this age were the things that turned your life one way or another.

She was nineteen when she decided to marry Sawyer's dad.

Sure, she had a wonderful son thanks to that fork in the road, but sometimes she did wonder if she hadn't met him or chose a better man to marry. What then? Sawyer was the best thing in her life, Bud wasn't all bad. Ugh. It was all her choices smacking her in the face. Why couldn't her son learn from her experience?

The air in the room felt wet, fetid even. She felt sick. She knew she needed to cool down and take a step back. What she did right now could sway her son's future. What if she said the wrong thing? Pushed on the wrong point?

"I need to get some air."

"Aunt Ali asked me to go out and set up the cabanas. I'm going to go do that. Can I have my phone back?"

"Okay." She handed him his phone, feeling the sting of defeat.

She wanted to fight. She wanted to yell. It felt, in that moment, like everything she had done for the first nineteen years of Sawyer's life had been a mistake. Sawyer was dropping out of college. Sawyer thought living on the beach was a great idea. Sawyer had no clue. And it turns out, neither did she.

Twenty-Nine

FAYE

Faye's problems were top of her mind when she discovered that Ali had new problems of her own.

While Faye was confronting Sawyer, Ali was confronting the fact that all her guests had up and left the cottages, even after all the work they had all done to get ready to open.

Faye needed to console Ali even while she knew her own life was off track in all directions.

Ali was not herself, not by a mile. She was as negative as Faye had ever seen her. She'd gone from loss to loss to loss in her mind.

Faye saw the opposite. She saw a woman so close to her dreams she just needed to grab them, but of course, maybe they were so close they were blinding her.

Faye listened. She let Ali feel what she needed to. Faye had never managed Ali and wouldn't try to start now. Her big sister could have a moment, and Faye would be there however Ali needed.

"I don't know. I thought I did everything, and now things are looking impossible," she said.

The two sat on the beach for the Grand Finale, which was missing the twelve people it was designed for. Ted, Katie, Jorge, and Didi made up their little group. The guests had evaporated, and with them, all her sister's high hopes. The latest disaster was plumbing in nature.

"Look, you can't blame yourself for a little bit of bad luck."

"I replaced the toilet. It's my fault—I should've had a plumber in, but it was working right. Ted even checked it. It was, but I'm not a plumber."

Faye wondered why Ted was involved at all. But she was trying to make things better, not worse.

Ted had wandered out to the beach. And sister time was over.

Ugh. Ted.

"Yeah, it looked good to me. But I mean, yeah, you really should have a professional for that kind of thing," he said.

Faye didn't hold back the hate in her eyes. If she had x-ray vision, she'd have incinerated Ted, so there would be nothing left but his New Balance tennis shoes. For once, though, he realized he was on dangerous ground with her and shut up. He searched the anemic group and found Katie.

"Katie, what you got there?"

Ted made himself scarce, just the way she liked it. Faye made a grumpy noise in the general direction of Ted as he walked away and toward Katie.

"Listen, I know you guys don't get along, but he's been really helpful," Ali said.

"I'm trying to be nice," Faye said. Then she plastered a crazy smile on her face. "See, nice."

Ali laughed at her comical, demented face. Well, that was something. She'd got Ali to laugh.

"I was melting down after that second incident today, and Ted helped."

"Are we discussing the same Ted? The Ted who doesn't know how to keep his..."

"Don't say that. I've not told Katie anything about it. I don't want her to overhear."

Faye didn't say what was really on her mind. She was saying all the wrong things with Sawyer; she didn't want to do the same with Ali.

Faye was hoping that something, anything, of what they were working on would just work out. She wished the old, capable Ali —the Ali who could do anything—would re-emerge right now. The Ali in front of her was defeated, discouraged, and sad. Faye was at a loss for how to fix anyone's life right now.

"I just...I hate to say it, but I'm afraid I might be squandering a lucrative opportunity for all three of us to make a huge amount of money by just selling the place."

Faye hated to hear this line of thought. "Don't forget, you'll only get half of a third of whatever this place goes for," Faye pointed out.

"At this point, half of a third of whatever we can get is better than half of a third of nothing," Ali replied.

Faye looked out to the water; the sun was hot, still, and it stung her eyes as it sank further into the waters of the gulf. The sand, too, felt like it was sizzling her skin.

It made her think of Sawyer. Where was he? Did he have sunscreen on? Ugh, she was overly babying him. She knew it. She also wished she had Bruce to help her. Sometimes, his old man's old-school wisdom had come in handy while raising her boy. She missed her dad at the strangest times. And for the weirdest reasons. She did not mention that he could have fixed that toilet, because that opened another can of worms.

Why in the world did he hide this from them?

Faye put her arm around her sister and squeezed her shoulders. Faye didn't really have answers. For Sawyer, for herself, or for Ali. The day had knocked the bluster out of her.

They sat for a moment, and after a little while, Katie and Ted decided to take a walk on the beach.

They interrupted Faye and Ali with an invite.

"Mom, Aunt Faye, join us? We're going to walk until the sunset."

Faye decided that if what Ali needed right now was Ted or time with her core family, then so be it. She wasn't going to cause friction. She silently vowed to just be here when the Ted thing blew up again. As she knew it had to.

"You go with them. Well, go with Katie," Faye said in Ali's ear. She squeezed her sister's hand.

"Thanks."

Ali stood up, and Faye watched her walk away. It shouldn't be weird to see Ali with Ted and Katie, but it left a bad taste in Faye's mouth. It felt like everything was going backward, not forward.

"Wow, this is the worst reaction to a sunset on Haven Beach that I've ever seen."

Faye nearly jumped out of the Adirondack chair.

She looked around and saw Rudy Palm Tree.

"Oh, hey," she said.

"Hi!"

"Did you forget you told me to come?"

"Actually, no. I just...we've had one of those bad days, you know?"

"I heard you lost all your guests."

"Yeah, it's very strange."

"I thought your sister was kind of experienced with the whole hospitality industry."

"She is, but..."

"What are the odds? I mean, two disasters in one day."

"Yeah, what are the odds?" Faye replied.

"It's almost like you've got a saboteur."

"What?"

"You know, someone doing it on purpose. If I were you, I would look at the security cameras."

Faye didn't even realize they had security cameras. Rudy pointed to several trained on the courtyard.

"When did those go up?"

"I think I mentioned it when I met you. A friend of mine was out here and put them up. He does doorbell cams and fancy security. Even did the next-door billionaire. He did this place a couple weeks before you got here. Smart to have."

"Ford Taylor? He did Ford Taylor's set up and The Sea Turtle?" That seemed like two ends of the budget spectrum.

"Yeah, he's got a range of stuff. I think your sister probably has an app or something on her phone to check. Motion sensitive, I'd guess."

She looked up at the courtyard cameras.

"That seems kind of paranoid," Faye said. Suspicion started to grow like a weed in her brain, though.

"Yeah, but I mean, one disaster is a disaster, bad luck, or a fluke. But two? Sounds like sabotage. I used to be in the military. We talk like that."

Rudy smiled at her. If she wasn't so worried about the idea that someone was messing with The Sea Turtle, she would have spent a moment appreciating how Rudy Palm Tree's smile was disarming as heck.

But she had bigger concerns right now.

Is someone deliberately ruining all of Ali's hard work?

Thirty

DIDI

Didi could barely keep up with all the improvements that Ali was making at The Sea Turtle. It was a testament to how hard she worked and how much she cared. Didi was so proud of Ali and Faye.

Things were moving so fast and in such a positive direction. On the one hand, it was wonderful. On the other hand, though, seeing how much had been accomplished by new blood here shined a light on the truth.

She and Jorge were really getting a little too old for this.

She watched Ali blossom as she took on the challenge of hospitality, organizing the spaces, and dealing with contractors.

Didi had to admit she was too tired after lunch to do the dozens of things on the list that Ali had posted in the office. Worse, she saw Jorge was too. He did not want to hear that. Jorge was always patient with her, except if she asked him if his hip was okay or suggested he might want to take a rest and let Sawyer carry all the cushions.

Jorge was mean as a snake when she said that he should slow down. Even though she saw him wince when he didn't know she was looking.

Faye saw it, too. Maybe she'd learned what to look for while taking care of ornery old Bruce Kelly in his final years.

While Faye was doing the landscaping work, she frequently asked Jorge and Didi for their opinions. It was glorious to be asked.

"So, the dune vegetation, what's the rule?"

Jorge piped up and identified native dune plants for Faye.

"And they have rules for trimming," Jorge pointed out.

"Because of the turtles?"

"Yes, the dune vegetation protects them and us from storms."

"No trimming at all?"

"You can, but there needs to be a permit."

Faye guided the two of them to the chairs Sawyer had placed near the dunes. Faye continued to talk about Sea Grapes and Wild Lime and Beach Sunflowers with Jorge.

"I'll apply for the vegetation trimming permit if you let me know what ones you want to trim," Jorge offered to Faye.

"No, no. I don't want you to be doing it," Faye said. "I need you to be supervising me. No job gets done well without a great foreman. I should know."

It was amazing to Didi that the little girl who had flowers in her hair the last time she saw her now had flowers in her life. Didi knew that Faye had spent most of her career following in Bruce Kelly's footsteps—she was a foreman, just like Bruce. But here, at the beach, that little girl who loved to pick flowers was blossoming.

Faye's son, Sawyer, was the biggest surprise of all. As much as she enjoyed Ali and Faye, it was Sawyer who really tickled her!

Getting to know Sawyer put a smile on her face.

The first day that Sawyer was there—running around, lifting things, moving things, cleaning things—he'd noticed some tile along the pool. "Where did that come from?" he'd asked.

Sawyer had no idea, but the answer to the tile question was loaded.

Didi had been careful. She knew that giving away the history of the tile could give away how much she knew about the history of the property. She knew that Cornwell Bennett Sr. had loved Arts and Crafts tile, and her father, Cornwell Bennett Jr., had paid for authentic and vintage tiles to be installed in that swimming pool. The tiles were no accident.

As the green cleared up in the water, Sawyer had been duly gob smacked by what the bottom of the pool revealed. The tiles were unique, hand-crafted, and vintage. And Sawyer was going to figure that out. Just like, eventually, the girls would uncover the story behind their inheritance. No matter how hard Didi tried to hide it. She thought of the documents she'd stolen. That would delay things, not stop them.

When it was safe to do so, Sawyer swam to the bottom of the pool. "Man, that's so unique," he'd said, emerging from the water. "I know I've seen something like that somewhere. Do you know how long this has been there?"

She'd tried to brush off his inquiries.

"Oh, it's a swimming pool, kiddo, don't be so impressed. It's Florida."

But she knew the tile was probably very impressive if you knew about that kind of thing. She knew her grandfather and her father had imbedded high-end art pieces all over The Sea Turtle. They were still there, if you knew where to look and what you were looking at.

"I will say we love a good ceramic tile. The Arts & Crafts Museum is about twenty minutes' drive," Didi had said, trying to tell Sawyer what she knew without telling him everything.

"No way! I'm totally taking that road trip."

No one had ever asked about the tile, but somehow Sawyer was very into it. It was hard not to brag about her grandfather's vision. But she didn't want to give away her secret. It could ruin everything she was now enjoying.

A few days later, Sawyer showed up poolside with a box of vintage tile.

"Sawyer, oh my gosh! Where did you find this?" Didi exclaimed.

"My mom doesn't like to talk about it," he said, his voice lowering. "I'm kind of the deep, dark secret in her family. I love ceramics. I love to make it. I love to research it. I love to restore it. It's my jam."

Didi let out a hearty laugh. She'd imagined a deep, dark secret that involved drugs or something. Sawyer was a surprising anomaly.

"Why is that a deep, dark secret?"

"Well," Sawyer began, "because my mom doesn't know that I want to do it as a career. I had a ceramics teacher in high school that just changed my life. I could bore you on this for hours."

Somehow, Sawyer felt comfortable talking to Didi about his dreams even though he felt he couldn't share those with anyone else, even his mother.

She understood.

Didi's dreams were coming true. Joetta's long-left-behind family was here. They were in the fold, even if they didn't know it.

"Well, if ceramics is your worst vice, I'd say you're nearly a saint," Didi said. "Show me how you're going to restore that one area."

Sawyer walked out to the porch, and he explained—first, where he found the tile; second, how he was going to fix the tile; and third, how if he were to open his own tile-making studio, he would include patterns inspired by Rookwood and Grueby and Batchelder-Wilson.

She didn't know any of those names but listened with rapt attention. She suspected her father and grandfather knew them personally.

What a thoughtful young man Sawyer was!

"Sawyer, your mom thinks you're...I think, what's the word... oh, a deadbeat? A stoner? A surfer, dude?" Didi teased.

"Yeah, she's a little off the mark," Sawyer said, chuckling. "But not that much off the mark. I do like surfing."

Didi lived her life with a dark, corrosive secret that she kept from this branch of her family out of loyalty to her past. The secret that she kept was heavy and seemed to be getting harder to hold up with every passing day.

Having Sawyer entrust her with, let's face it, a good secret, made her heart sing.

Jorge continued to nag her about coming clean, about telling the girls what really happened, but she knew in her heart that if she did, all of this would go away.

The girls would rightly be so angry that they would never speak to her again. So, she kept it quiet and enjoyed her new bond with Sawyer.

And thanks to Sawyer, the vintage pool tile was looking brand new!

Thirty-One

ALI

To say Ali was at a low point would be an understatement. Not since the days right after her father's funeral had she felt so rudderless. Everything she thought she knew seemed to be slipping through her fingers.

She'd worked so hard to have the food and the lodging perfect, and yet it had blown up in her face.

The last two weeks had played out completely differently than she'd imagined. Ali needed to regroup, start a list, make calls, and fix things, but she just didn't seem to know where to start after all that had happened.

She was sitting in the office of The Sea Turtle when Ted walked in.

A month ago, she'd have had to steel herself to be in his presence. Right now, she was glad to see him.

Ted had helped her clean up both of those messes.

He'd even jumped in front of the macho man of the Bowman Family when he started yelling right in Ali's face.

And she'd always thought Ted was a complacent parent. He let her do the work and worry about everything so he could swoop in during chaos and say, "Calm down."

But he'd brought Katie down here because he didn't want their daughter to drive by herself. That was something she would have suggested if she'd been there when Katie was proposing it. He was concerned for their daughter and took action to help. Plus, he'd helped Ali with her car after it got smashed. And it was Ted who'd told her to get out of the car in the first place. She couldn't ever forget that.

This was a new side of him. He was, maybe, starting to realize what he'd lost.

She was feeling vulnerable but also grateful for Ted.

Ted sat down across from her in the little office.

Even the office space had improved since Ali got there. She'd put a dry-erase board on the wall, and she'd put up calendars and schedules. She'd organized the keys for the different rooms. She was in the midst of researching electronic entry systems. Still, now she wondered if any of it was really going to happen. Was investing any more capital a good idea?

"I need to— I meant to tell you, thank you for helping me with all this stuff." She was a big enough person to say thank you.

"You're welcome," Ted replied.

"I have a mess on my hands, but you've been a real help during the chaos this week."

"It's no problem. The thing is...maybe this isn't the time, maybe it is. I guess there's not a right time. But what I need to say is that I owe you an apology."

Ali didn't say anything.

She searched back into her memory. She wasn't sure if she'd ever received an apology from Ted. He was always right. Ted was always sure. Ted was professorial, and a lot of Ted's advice over the years had proved useful to Ali. She was sure she wouldn't have become the assistant manager of the Frogtown Center without him. He'd pushed her to do more than just administrative assistant work. He'd told her how to take credit for her accomplishments, and she'd risen up the ladder.

But the words *I'm sorry* were not words that the professor ever used.

"You're sorry." She repeated it, just to be sure.

"Yes, I'm sorry that I had an affair. It was a midlife crisis. It was stupid. I was a fool, and you had every right—every right—to leave. I promise it will never happen again."

Ali was shocked. She didn't know if she wanted the apology until she heard it. A gasp was all that came out of her mouth.

"What I'm saying is, I want you to take me back. I'll do anything."

"Ted, that's not..." Ali paused, unsure of her own words. "I think it might be too late."

"It's never too late," Ted said. "Look how well we worked together this last week. The two of us together with our kids—there's no stopping us."

Ted put a hand across the desk on top of Ali's. Her heartbeat seemed way too fast as it drummed in her chest.

Ali felt an impulse to recoil. But she stayed still.

They had more than twenty years together. That was something. That deserved something. Didn't it?

"We made two great kids. Can you imagine what our grandchildren will be like?"

Ali laughed. She could imagine. She wasn't ready to be a Gigi just yet, but she did think about it. She did dream about family events right outside the office in the courtyard. She thought of barefoot weddings on the beach. Of building sandcastles.

Ted pressed on and painted another picture. One that scared her.

"We can fix this. You don't want a life with our kids or grandkids splitting time between two places for every holiday. Plus, once our kids get married, they'd split between us and then their future in-laws. You'd never see them, or you'd get a sliver of time. It doesn't have to be that way."

Ali hadn't thought about that. In her future she thought of her kids and theoretical grandchildren being with her, not Ted. Ted was the bad guy. But of course, they didn't know that. If she never told them why she left him, maybe *she* was the bad guy. Did protecting Ted mean she'd lose out on time with her children and her possible future grandchildren? It chilled her to the bone to think of that future.

Still, Ali needed to be strong.

"That's true," she admitted. "I would hate that, but that was not a reason to forgive you."

"Look," Ted said, "you don't have to answer me today, but I just want you to know that I know I messed up. And I won't mess up again. And I'll help you out of this mess."

He indicated that the mess was the office and the resort. She didn't like that. It wasn't a mess. Well, it wasn't until this week.

"Think about how much fun we had on the beach the other day with our Katie girl. I'm aware that it's also my fault we haven't done a lot of vacations together. I think we need to change that."

Ali found herself agreeing with Ted. She also found herself somewhat relieved because this was familiar. This was safe. Maybe this was the way things were supposed to go.

Thirty-Two

FAYE

It was early morning on Haven Beach.

Ali and Faye hadn't had time this week to do anything besides handle one crisis after another. But now, with an empty resort, Ali suggested they get up early and walk together, like they used to in their Old Orchard neighborhood.

Faye knew Ali was at a crossroads. Heck, so was she! You thought you knew where you were in midlife, only to be knocked off your feet and forced to start again.

"I need to get your take on some things I'm thinking about."

Faye was so glad the two of them could finally connect and that Ali was opening up a little.

They both ditched their flip-flops and walked on the cool sand on a relatively deserted beach. They passed other older beachgoers walking like they were. The beach in the morning was for seasoned travelers, not toddlers with sandcastles.

"I have made quite a mess of things," Ali sighed as they set off.

"You did not."

"Well, I should have had a plumber. I should have inspected for bugs. I tried to do way too much on my own."

"That's a typical Ali move."

"My point is, I'm trying to avoid making one more big mistake."

Faye wanted desperately to fix everything. Sawyer's entire life. Ali's relationship with Henry. And darn it all, she could not stop thinking about ways to fix The Sea Turtle Inn. Even though that was supposed to be Ali's mission.

"Girl, you're too hard on yourself. This isn't a 'just add water' resort. There's a little trial and error."

"No, I'm gambling with our futures, and I think it's selfish. But that's not what I want to tell you. I mean, it is, but also—"

"—Okay, sorry. I was distracted by how stupid your idea that you're bad at hotels because of one bum week."

"Right, okay, well, I'm thinking of getting back with Ted."

Whoa, there it is.

Faye stopped walking. Her feet sank a little into the sand. Her heart sank a lot.

Faye felt like Ali had completely forgotten everything she'd just learned about Ted. She probably should have tread lightly. Tact would have been the way to go, but this was her sister, and Faye was fresh out of b.s.

"That's a terrible idea."

"He said he was sorry, and he talked about how he would change. Things would change. And honestly, I'm not doing so hot here. I'm about to lose all our money on this pipe dream," Ali said, then rattled off a laundry list of other justifications.

Again, Faye chose honesty. That's what sisters were for: the truth. If Ali had a two-inch chin hair she'd missed, Faye would let her know. And Ted was that. Despite them knowing he could show up and ruin things, he'd been able to show up and ruin things.

So, Faye was honest: "He said he was sorry for being a serial cheater. Did you forget that it wasn't just that one time? He did it over and over. You only *caught* him that one time."

Ali put her hands on her ears. She was in denial. She had convinced herself that things weren't as bad as they clearly were, not with The Sea Turtle, but with the slime ball that was Ted Harris.

"I know. I know. But...Katie and Tye. They deserve better than having to go two places every holiday and—"

"What? Holidays? Stop right there! They're adults or nearly so. You need to live your life and not what they think your life ought to be. And two places? Holidays? That's you going out there and manufacturing future problems."

"Well, Bud's out of the picture. You and Sawyer don't have that issue."

"Sawyer, yeah, well, he's on my last nerve. We are not on a good foot. Let's leave him out of this."

Faye took her hands and put them on her big sister's shoulders.

She took a breath, and she poured out her best advice. Her sister had been in a marriage her entire adult life. Of course, she was going to blink in the final moments before her divorce. It wasn't a surprise, but it was a mistake.

"You're scared. I get it. Change is so hard. I'm in that same mode with you right now. Trying to keep Sawyer on track, trying to understand where I fit now that I am unemployed and don't have my job at the plant, I get it. We're in a season that we just don't know what's going to happen next. But I think you're operating from a place of fear. And that's not you."

"I am afraid. You're right. But I even failed at figuring out how we came into this place. I mean, it's from Mom, but how did Mom have it? What if we shouldn't have it at all? What if Mom, in classic Mom style, cursed us with this?"

"Cursed? No. Not possible."

"I have no idea how any of this happened, but here I am, living some life that seems fake. Like an imposter. Who is this person trying to live here in Florida on a beach?"

It was so odd to Faye that her beautiful and perfect and ridiculously competent big sister had imposter syndrome, but there it was.

"Do me two favors before you decide to forgive and forget with Ted."

"Depends on the favors." Ali narrowed her eyes at Faye.

"I need you to visit Henry. Tell him your decision. He has a crush on you and gave you space and helped you feel at home here. You owe that to him. And second. Well. I need to see the security cameras login."

"What?"

"I need you to agree to these things. No questions asked. Remember, you owe Sawyer and me?" Faye gently shook Ali's shoulders.

She smiled. "Fine, I'll text you the security camera stuff. But really, Henry?"

"I think you need lunch at the Seashell Shack, and I think you need to see that you're building a life here. One your kids would be lucky to be a part of. And Ted? He's the past."

Ali took a deep breath and looked out to the water. The surf was quiet this morning. Each wave gently rolled in, touched their toes, and rolled out.

Ali looked at Faye and nodded yes. "Fine, I'll do it for you. But I want you to be prepared. We're going to need to sell this place before the Yelp reviews for our two disaster guests get posted."

"Oh, I'm prepared. Don't you worry!"

Faye was banking on two hunches. One, that Henry was the better man and Ali just needed to be reminded. And two—well, she didn't even want to think about the hunch and what the security cameras might reveal.

Thirty-Three

ALI

Ali promised Faye. But that didn't mean she had to like it.

It was true, she did like Henry. She knew Faye was right about that. At the very least, she had to tell her friend what was on her mind. She probably owed the same conversation to Erica too.

Erica and Henry were her lifelines here, and they were the same. Henry was her friend, just like Erica. She kissed him that one time as a little experiment. Nothing more. She didn't need to be so nervous.

Except she was.

She walked the few feet down the beach from The Sea Turtle to the Seashell Shack.

It was early; still, the lunch crowd would swell in an hour or so. She had the sweatshirt Henry had given her neatly washed and folded. She needed to give it back.

The majority of the seating at the Seashell Shack was outside. Umbrellas placed in the center of sturdy wooden picnic tables were arranged in rows extending from the back of the restaurant. There was indoor seating, but who wanted to do that when you could be on the deck or on the beach itself? Cornhole games and three volleyball nets also provided constant fun for people on vacation.

Maybe that was it. Maybe Ali was living in a fantasy land of a vacation mindset. Reality had set in, and she needed to deal with it. Her life wasn't on the beach, it never had been.

Ali needed to get back to her life in Old Orchard, to the Old Orchard house she'd restored inch by inch, mostly by herself.

By herself. Ted was not handy. That was the weird thing about the last few days. He'd pitched in on handyman tasks that she'd needed to be done. But probably just to get on her good side.

The recollection of the old Ted put a chink in her armor. She was sure she was here to tell Henry that she was going to be leaving. That this was a fluke. Or an extended bout of self-care. Or the living out of a fantasy everyone has when they visit the beach: *Maybe I could live here...*

The reality was no, no, you can't.

Henry could; she couldn't.

Henry was at home at this restaurant. He had an easy rapport with the customers and a gentle style with his staff. It made eating at the Seashell Shack the perfect relaxed vibe.

Ali did not feel relaxed. She felt dread.

Henry came out onto the back deck, and a smile lit up his very handsome face. His salt-and-pepper hair and a few wrinkles around the eyes were the only way you'd know he wasn't still playing baseball.

She'd looked it up. He'd downplayed his days as a ballplayer, but he was good. He was in the majors for five years. That was amazing. He'd been a Detroit Tiger along with being a Toledo Mud Hen. He'd been on other teams, too. But he didn't brag about it. In fact, he did the opposite. Most guys would brag about the littlest things or have a hot car to compensate for not being a professional baseball player.

She stopped herself from that line of thought.

Ted had a car that he drove to impress. But she was trying to be generous in her thoughts about Ted. She'd need to be if this was going to work. She would have to forgive. That might be easier than forgetting. Forgetting was the real trick.

"I'm so glad to see you, about time you visited. Let me get you set up for lunch!"

She didn't want lunch. And he'd likely want her out of there, anyway, once she'd said her piece. He should give seats to better customers. She was a bucket dipper; she'd only gotten from Henry and given nothing. *Ugh.*

"I wanted to tell you something," Ali said.

She quickly began to doubt what she wanted to say. A few seconds ago, she was thinking it would be hard to forget the bad aspects of being married to Ted.

But right now, as soon as she saw Henry, Ted and all thoughts of him evaporated. *Ted who? Ted where?*

"I'm here to, uh, return this sweatshirt." That was not why she was there. She was there to...*why was she there again?*

"What? No way, you're good at advertising. No one looks as good as you do in that thing. I won't allow you to return it. In fact, I'd like to pay you to wear it." He gave her a wink.

"Yes, the five-foot-three model, that's me. I remember."

"You're put together just right. Now you want to go inside or outside? You have a little sunburn on your nose, maybe inside? I want to hear all about your plans for week two. I know you hit a bump with week one, but we all do."

In this one exchange, Henry showed he cared about her, really noticed her, wanted to know about her business, and—judging by the flirting—maybe wanted to be with her.

Ali threw her plans out the window.

She stepped forward, put her hand on Henry's shoulder, and stretched up as high as she could while also pulling him down to her level.

She kissed Henry Hawkins on the lips!

She didn't do it lightly or halfway. It was a full-on kiss. She also included a run of her fingers through his salt-and-pepper hair. The resulting *zing* went from her lips to her flip-flops.

Ali let Henry go and looked him in the eye.

He shook his head as though she'd hit him with a line drive.

"Well, that was unexpected. I knew you were a good kisser, but broad daylight, quite the bold move, Ali Harris."

"Kelly, the name's Ali Kelly. And I just needed to figure something out."

"And did you?"

"I did. I may not know how to run a hotel, but I do know I like you. I like you better than my almost ex-husband. Do you feel the same?"

"I feel the same, times ten. I don't like your ex one bit. I was just staying out of your way while you, what did you call it? Figured it out."

"Got it. I have to go."

"Not having lunch?"

"No, but I'll see you at the Grand Finale, and I expect you most nights, got it?"

"Yes, I do, Ali Kelly."

Ali wasn't going to be getting back with Ted. Not by a mile.

The rest of it? Well, she'd figure that out, too.

Thirty-Four

FAYE

Sawyer was by the pool, doing something, again, with tiles. He was always fidgeting with the tiles.

Faye had Ali's code for the security cameras, but she didn't know how to find the recordings she needed.

Sawyer knew how to do stuff on the phone. She needed his help.

They hadn't talked much since he'd announced his life plan to her after she spied on him. Faye didn't want to fight. She wanted him to be smart. But right now, she wanted him to help her, so she decided she did owe him an apology.

"I'm sorry I snooped. But I need you to help me snoop some more."

"Um, well, who are you snooping on this time? Katie? Your sister? The Russians?"

"No, no. I'm snooping for my sister. Not against her."

"Mom, you're very good at justifying invading people's privacy."

"I'm sorry, I truly am. And I have permission this time."

She stopped for a moment and realized she'd said she was sorry without any feeling or sincerity.

Sawyer had grown a lot in the last year. Maybe knowing what you wanted to do and what you didn't was part of that. She couldn't live his life for him. No matter how she wanted him to learn from her mistakes or Bud's, that's not how it worked. The wisdom of a parent wasn't hers to pass on. No parent could. You just had to wait, and hope.

"Sawyer, I really am sorry. Snooping was a mad move. Left over from when you were in high school and skipped with Tye to go to the quarry."

That incident caused quite an uproar; she wished that was the level of problem they had. Lately every problem seemed life altering. *Skipping school, ha, amateur hour.*

"I'm not a kid." He wasn't a kid and maybe he was more adult than she'd given him credit for.

"But I suspected you were lying, and you were." She defended herself but it felt hollow.

"I know, but that's because you weren't listening."

That hurt because he was right. She hadn't listened to one bit of his plan. She'd made him listen to her plans for him.

"I am going to try to be better, okay? I want to really hear your plans and what you're thinking. But right now, well, right now, I'm messing in someone else's business. Not yours. See, that's progress."

"Ugh, okay, fine. Whose life are you arranging now?"

Faye got out her phone. She knew she'd need to look at the video on her phone but just didn't know how.

"I have a code to see the security cameras that Aunt Ali set up. She gave me the codes, so see? All above board. I want to see what the cameras recorded for a specific time period."

"Easy. First up, you need the app. The footage will be stored in their cloud."

"Uh, cloud?" Faye fumbled around her phone for a second, and Sawyer lost patience.

"Give it to me." He downloaded the app and then put in the code Faye had for the cameras.

"Ah, there it is." She watched the camera that showed the two beach cottages that had been rented.

The camera only recorded when there was motion. Ali, Katie, Faye, Sawyer—all of them moved in and out of the frame. Then, the Bowmans and Deans checked in. She watched a little more and saw a lizard that was twice the size of the geckos.

"Wow, look at that guy!" Faye said out loud, momentarily thrown off the scent of her actual quarry.

"What are you looking for specifically? We can put time parameters in," Sawyer offered.

Faye snapped back to her mission.

She also hesitated. Did she want to tell Sawyer if her hunch proved true? Or did she owe it to Ali to decide what to do once she had the facts? Faye decided, for once, to play it close to the vest instead of blurting.

"I'm going to have to let your aunt tell you if this shows what I think it might."

"Okay...so, are we good?"

"Do you mean with this app or universally?"

"Universally," Sawyer said.

Faye looked up from the phone and at her handsome son. Where was the baby again? It all went by so fast. This man in front of her had taken his shift driving across the country, watched out for her when they were in the Deliverance Rest Stop, and had thrown himself into helping make The Sea Turtle ready for the world.

She had to trust him to lead his own life. Even if she did still have to remind him about sunscreen, constantly.

She decided to be honest.

"I'm scared; that's the main issue. I'm scared you're throwing your future away."

"Mom, I'm not Bud, you know?"

"I don't think you are." That was a lie. She was worried about that. She was worried that all of Sawyer's dawdling about school was because he was a deadbeat or had deadbeat DNA from his dad.

"I have watched you work and work and work," Sawyer said calmly. "I have that in me more than anything else."

"If you were working, you'd work on school."

"No, it's not that. I want to work, but I want to work on being an artist."

Faye winced. No one in their family was an artist. This sounded like a road to starvation and homelessness.

"What does that even mean? Like wearing a beret and painting the Eiffel Tower?"

"Mom, you know it doesn't. What I want to be is a ceramics artist. And that's the job I've lined up. I'm going to apprentice a local company here; they make decorative tile."

"I like the sound of apprentice, but can't you be an apprentice welder or plumber or something more, uh, substantial? I mean, if you don't want to go to college, at least get into the trades."

"Actually, I do want to go to college. Here."

"Really?"

"Let me show you something. Look at the bottom of the pool."

"You better not push me in."

"I'm not going to push you in." Sawyer pointed into the watery blue. "See those tiles, and then see how they come here, to the edge. What do you think?"

"They're gorgeous. It's amazing what you can see when it's not green."

"Yeah, right, but do you notice any difference between the tiles?"

Faye looked hard. She felt like she was missing something. "No, I guess I don't. I'm sorry, honey, if you asked me about native plants or how to start garlic, maybe, but I just don't have a good eye."

"Yeah, you do, because that was the right answer; there is very little difference. I worked hard to be sure of it."

"Wait, you *made* these tiles?"

"Yep, that's the apprenticeship and the schooling. I'm going to go to this art tile place and work as a glazer and, meanwhile, get a degree from the University of South Florida. They have a path where I can combine my art degree with marketing so I can learn how to sell my work."

Faye's mouth dropped open.

Sawyer really did have a plan. And it included actual schooling. He'd done research and had answers for the questions that had plagued her.

"Mom, a fly is going to go in there."

She snapped her mouth shut and then laughed at the phrase she used to say to Sawyer when his mouth dropped open.

"I'm just so sorry. I was pushing you into what I thought was the right path."

"I know, Mom, I know. But I gotta do my path. Get it?"

"I get it. I mean, slowly, I get it. I'm not as smart as you."

And then the reality of what he was saying sunk in.

"You're going to move down here permanently? How will you live? I told you, this whole hotel thing, it might not last. It might be that you need to find a place." A million contingencies popped into Faye's head.

"Mom, it's cool. Didi and Jorge have room. There's space here. I'm not moving to Florida by myself. It's practically family here everywhere I turn."

Faye reached up and hugged her son. He was grown. This was a grown decision, following his own path and setting up his own life.

She was half elated for him and half sad. He didn't need her anymore. And he was going to live here, not in Ohio.

She didn't share the bitter part of bittersweet with him. She just hugged him. She didn't want to hold him back; she wanted him to grow up. To thrive. He was working to do just that.

Faye knew this was the goal, setting your kids up so they could stand on their own and find their own dreams.

But what came next for her? She'd be alone all the time. Ali had moved. Sawyer was moving. Her life would be so different in Toledo.

That was the bitter, and she swallowed it quietly. She owed her son support, and she also owed him the freedom from her fears. Faye kept them to herself. She patted his head.

"Okay, skedaddle. I need to get back to my spy craft."

Sawyer popped up from their hug. "Katie and I are going to the Mahuffer's at Indian Rocks. Don't wait up."

"Wear sunscreen!"

"It's sunset."

"Still."

She watched her son away with big, confident strides. She was so proud of him. She was scared for him. She was scared for herself. And she was tired of all this drama.

Faye shook her head and knew that, in her case, the best remedy for melancholy was a project.

The project was the security camera. She believed none of the disasters at The Sea Turtle were Ali's mistakes. Now, it was time for the proof.

Faye used Sawyer's instructions and typed in two very specific times.

When her hunch was proved right, she yelled, "AH-HA!"

Luckily, no one was sitting by the pool, or they'd have thought she'd gone round the bend.

What the cameras showed may not have been admissible in a

court of law, but it could be enough to pull Ali out of Denial River!

She hoped.

Thirty-Five

ALI

They sat in The Sea Turtle office.

It wasn't ideal having Faye there when she needed to tell Ted that their reconciliation wasn't happening. She wasn't sure what would come next with The Sea Turtle, but she did know that moving back in with Ted wasn't the direction she was headed. But before Ali could tell Ted they weren't getting back together, Faye had insisted Ted and Ali meet her in the office.

"So, I asked to meet you both because I want to show you something," said Faye.

"You know, I have a meeting in a few minutes. I really don't have time right now," Ted said.

Ali looked at Ted in confusion. *What meeting could he possibly have down here?*

Faye stood up and angled her phone out so they could see her screen. She pressed an arrow, and a video came up.

"What are we looking at?" Ted asked.

"This is the security camera that Ali set up before we all got down here."

"I didn't know you had cameras," Ted said to Ali. He shifted in his chair.

Was that sweat on his upper lip?

"I had them placed so they didn't interfere with the cottage beachy feel," Ali explained.

"Good plan," Faye said.

"Thanks," Ali said.

Faye seemed victorious, ready to pounce or something. Ali hated feeling out of the loop and she was completely out of it right now.

"I'm sure you know what I found, Ted," Faye said.

Ali had no idea what Faye had found.

"So, you're Magnum P.I. now?" Ted sneered at Faye. Faye sent back a face that could have been eight-year-old Faye in elementary school. Ali was too busy for this, whatever this was.

"Ali, take a look here." Faye pointed to the screen and tapped play.

The video screen showed the front of the Strawberry Hideaway. The cottage the Deans were staying in. It showed Ted delivering the food to the front deck of the Strawberry. He put the food on the table and then took something out of his pocket. It was a bag. Ted's body language in the video was almost twitchy, like he didn't really want to touch the bag.

"What the heck is that?" Ali asked.

"Spiders, I'd bet a million bucks. That's what is in that bag that's giving him the heebie jeebies. He's the one that put them on the breakfast food. Look at him mess with the wrappers."

"I did not! You're off your rocker, as usual."

"I'm not. Explain this then."

She clicked on a different video and put her phone out to face Ted and Ali.

In that one, he entered the Mango Mansion with toilet paper rolls in his hand.

"Faye, I asked him to deliver that," Ali told her. "That isn't proof he clogged the toilets."

"It's not proof he didn't, either. This is exactly when the Bowman family was at Busch Gardens."

"I've had it!" Ted said. "I will not be accused of petty crime by Inspector Badger over here. What possible reason could I have to do all that, anyway?"

Faye turned on Ted like she was performing a climactic monologue in an Agatha Christie movie.

"You've been undermining my sister since you got here. You want this place sold. Why not make it impossible for Ali to get guests? Seems to me that falls right in line with the plan to stay married to my sister and bleed her dry."

"I came here for your niece, my daughter, and because I do regret my behavior. But you are not the person I have to convince."

Ted and Faye looked at Ali. And then they started hurling insults at each other.

"Cheater!"

"Liar!"

"Man-hating shrew!"

This was nuts. Ali worked hard to keep people from fighting. She prided herself on making sure everyone got along. She intervened in all family discord. But here she was in the middle of a near fistfight between Ted and Faye.

Nothing she could do would smooth this over!

The two of them were shouting at each other, and the fight was near top volume. Ali felt like she was having an out-of-body experience.

All her life, she'd managed to keep the peace. She'd done it with her parents. She'd done it between Bruce and her sisters. She'd done it at the Frogtown.

Why? Was it so bad if other people fought?

Would Faye or Ted die if they got in an argument? Would she? No. No they wouldn't.

She was done! Let them fight. Let them hate each other. It wasn't her relationship to fix.

These two weren't her job. It wasn't her job to make Ted likable or stop Faye from blurting whatever it was Faye wanted to blurt.

It was only her job to be herself. More specifically, to be true to herself.

That's when she cut through the name-calling with her own strong voice.

"Ted, about that, I am *not* going back with you. I appreciate all your help, and I agree. This video isn't...well, Faye, I just mean— Ted wouldn't do that."

But as she said it, she wondered if she believed it.

It was certainly possible that Ted saw dollar signs, not a happy reconciliation. Her quitting on this idea and getting back with him would be exactly what he needed to maybe get millions.

Faye wanted to punch Ted in the mouth. Ali could see that. She also felt like an idiot for nearly getting back with Ted. *This* was Ted. It was one of the things she hated about him. He was hot-tempered and selfish. A lifetime of always capitulating to him, and before him, to Bruce, and before that, to her own mother's issues —suddenly, it all seemed to press down on Ali.

One visit from Ted and she was ready to quit this new adventure and go back to her predictable life in Toledo?

No! She'd taken the road less traveled here, and she'd have to navigate whatever that meant. The terrain wasn't smooth, but the view was spectacular. She had to be strong enough to keep going on this path.

Ted stood there, looking confused, angry, and maybe even like he understood he'd lost something.

A knock on the screen door interrupted the drama. Faye and Ted remembered themselves a little. It was one thing to lose your cool in front of family, but a random person at the door you'll likely never see again. Yeah, better be on your best behavior.

But Ali was relieved. The stranger had interrupted the family fight freight train before it pulled into an out-brawl station.

"You the owner?" the man at the door said.

"Yes, yes, I am." Ali stood up and walked around from behind her little desk. The man handed her a manila folder. "Yeah, here's the inspection report."

"What?"

"Yeah, this is for the inn next door. Building compliance report. This place is shut down until further notice."

"What?"

"Safety hazard until you prove mitigation efforts are underway at that structure." The inspector turned and left without more explanation.

"I didn't even know they did an inspection," Ali said, scanning the documents she'd been handed.

"Yeah, they did. When you were out running errands, I scheduled it. I let them in. It didn't take long," Ted said.

Ali was livid that he hadn't said a word about it. That he'd just done what he always did: ignored that she was in charge!

"Ted, you're the worst, the absolute worst," Faye said. "But I'll let you two talk. I've said my piece about this piece of—"

"—Faye!"

"Yeah, yeah, high road and all."

"You couldn't find the high road if it hit you in the—"

"—Ted!"

Ali had her hands up, palm toward each of her sparring family members. Ted was her family. Even if she was about to cut him loose from her life, for good this time.

Faye looked at Ali, and Ali put on her best BIG SISTER face. *Enough of this nonsense.*

Faye caught Ali's vibe. She'd done what she could to help Ali see Ted's flaws.

"Why don't you give me that report?" Faye said. "I'm used to reading that kind of thing."

Ali handed Faye the documents, and she watched her little sister stick her tongue out at Ted as she walked out of the office.

Ali used her index fingers to rub her temples. She was developing a headache. She tried to process the new information that Ted might have caused all her problems this week. It was awful, but in a way, it changed nothing. She'd already decided something before she'd seen what Faye was showing them. She'd seen a glimpse of her future with Ted and without him. And she'd made a choice.

"Look, I think Faye gets carried away," she said to Ted after a pause. "I am going to choose to believe you had nothing to do with the issues we had. And I truly am grateful for your help with the Jeep. But we're not getting back together, and I'm not selling this place."

"Did you not hear him? They're shutting down the inn."

"No one is booked there, so that's not really an issue. Yet." She opened the desk drawer and pulled out a similar-looking manila envelope.

Ali had documents of her own.

She opened the envelope and pulled out the paperwork. She showed the papers to Ted.

"You signed?"

"I signed, and you'll do the same. There's a current value on this property. I will be paying you one-half of one-third of its current value, and uh, minus the value you see there on the inn. I'll be subtracting the value of the inn, since it's shut down. So, uh, here. I'll need you to initial that little bit."

Ali neatly scratched out the number on the document that had a value for the inn. She wrote a big fat zero. And then she spelled it out.

"Looks like you sort of screwed yourself over on the value, by getting the inn shut down."

"Unless you sell."

"No one is buying in Florida right now. Don't you watch the news? Sorry to say, well, sorry for you."

"I will not sign. I do not agree to this."

"You will, actually. I've even got my checkbook here. I'll write it right now."

"$75,000 is nothing."

"You also get the house I made for you. That house is worth a lot in Toledo's market."

"I'm not selling it. It's convenient for the university."

"Whatever you like, it's all yours."

"I'm not doing this."

"Okay, take it or leave it, but if you leave it, I'll call the police on your little sabotage," Ali told him, waving the phone at Ted to remind him of what just happened. "Oh, and one more thing, I will be telling Katie why we're divorcing."

"You wouldn't."

"I don't want to. She thinks I am being selfish, leaving you for one mistake. She doesn't know about all the mistakes. I do. I had forgotten that for a minute. I believed that maybe we could be old folks enjoying grandchildren together. But that isn't happening. And trust me, if I tell the kids the truth, they likely won't be too conflicted on who to visit at Christmas."

"You're making a huge mistake. This place is going under. You'll go bankrupt and then try to sell, what, a hotel with structural issues that can't keep a guest for more than one night?"

"Ted, what I do with this place is my decision," Ali replied, noticing how quickly Ted's relationship with his children had taken that backseat to the financial matters. "The decision is mine and my sisters, and you don't have to worry about it, okay?"

Ali had some of the cash inheritance from her dad's insurance and the sale of his home to pay off Ted.

It irked her that he was the one coming out on top financially, but the money was worth a clean break. She needed a clean break.

And she was betting on her future. She was betting that she could make The Sea Turtle dream come true.

Ted grabbed the divorce paper; he took a pen off her desk and signed it. If you can sign in a huff, that's how Ted wielded the ballpoint pen.

She'd thought they'd be mailing stuff back and forth, but no need. It was done. They'd both signed.

"Tell Katie when you see her, we're leaving tomorrow at noon."

"Got it. And Ted, my new boyfriend is going to be at the Grand Finale tonight, so maybe you'd be better skipping it."

At that moment, Ali channeled Faye, and what she wanted to say, she said! Out loud.

Take that, Ted.

Thirty-Six

DIDI

Didi and Ali had a moment before everyone arrived for the Grand Finale.

"So, Ted and I signed the papers."

"You did? I thought you were thinking of reconciling with him."

"No, yeah, well, I was, a little, but I was reminded about what went wrong. And I was backsliding into a place of fear or comfort."

"No shame in that. Change is so hard," Didi reassured Ali. "How did Katie take it?"

"She was okay, blames me though. I am the one who left, after all."

"Did you tell her why you left?"

"No, I lied," Ali said. "I still can't bring myself to destroy her image of her dad."

"You won't need to; it will happen on its own. That's my prediction."

Didi understood more than Ali realized. Ali had lied to protect her family. Didi knew very well what that felt like.

Ali waved to Jorge, and he joined them.

"You two sit, take a load off. It's just us tonight for the festivities."

Didi and Jorge felt like a King and Queen. Sawyer did the heavy lifting. Ali poured the cocktails. Faye was so funny, recounting the way they'd given Ted the boot.

Ali shushed Faye when Katie appeared.

Katie was a beauty. She looked a little like Didi's own grand-daughter. That thought caused a cascade of guilt.

How was she going to get the family in one room? Katie and her own sweet Rori would take one look at each other and see that they were clearly of the same gene pool!

Didi took a rather large gulp of wine at the thought.

She was sad that it was Faye and Katie's last night but still couldn't believe her luck that this family had found her, sort of.

Jorge kicked her chair with his foot.

"What?"

"You planning on spilling the beans to them? Now would be a very good time."

"Jorge Rivera, keep your voice down."

Ali heard them and asked the question. "Spill the beans on what?"

"Nothing, just, uh..." Didi nearly did it. She nearly told them all the secrets she'd been helping hide for decades.

But just then Faye came up and patted her shoulder, then kissed her on the head.

This was too good to risk. She couldn't let this slip away.

"Uh, spill the beans on the neighbor. I saw him today. And I invited him, but of course, he's got a busy dance card."

"You are kidding me; you invited Ford Taylor to the Grand Finale?" Katie knew exactly who the fancy designer renovating an even fancier house down the beach was.

"I did. He puts on his designer flip-flops on one foot at a time, doesn't he?"

"Didi, you're a hoot. I love you," Faye said, and then Erica and Henry showed up with snacks. Didi loved snacks. She loved this gathering.

She watched Ali greet Henry. She looked at their eyes, and she swore if Katie wasn't here the two of them would have embraced.

Wow. The things you miss when you run into Moe's to get snacks.

Ali was blossoming here. She remembered the little girl in Toledo that she'd visited. The little girl who took care of Joetta when Joetta was a total mess.

Didi didn't want any of these bubbles to burst. But the weight of the lie...she knew she couldn't keep holding it forever.

As they laughed and appreciated the beauty of today's flavor of sunset, mostly blue and pink, with the sun slightly hidden behind a light gray layer of clouds, Didi rotated her feet.

Her legs were rather swollen today, and she had a little ache in her shoulder.

She just needed to rest, enjoy this moment, and worry about this secret another day.

Thirty-Seven

ALI

While the sunsets at Haven Beach stunned, overwhelmed, and dazzled, Ali had of late felt the showstoppers were for the guests. She loved that she could give them and her friends and family the perfect sunset experience.

But the sunrise was for her. No matter what happened next, guests or family, Ali made a promise to herself to walk this beach and breathe deeply of the salt air every morning. This morning was the first time she put her feet onto the sand as Ali Kelly, not Ali Harris.

She knew who she'd become was a product of both of those names but decided that Ali Kelly was her name after signing those papers.

The sand was cold in the morning, a stark contrast to how it felt underfoot in the middle of the day when sometimes you had to run to get to the water and cool your feet.

Ali walked along the beach, passing the occasional jogger and watching the little white birds run back and forth into the surf.

She'd learned they were called Sanderlings, and if Ali didn't have a busy day ahead, she easily could have spent the day watching the shorebirds live their lives in sync with the waves.

Occasionally, she would see a shell worthy of her collection. She'd started to develop her own categorization system for her beachy finds. Some were flawless, others of a unique color, and still a third category emerged of shells that were different and alien from the others. Any one of those distinguishing characteristics would compel her to bend down and carefully pick up the shell. Lately, she'd been putting the shells on the deck railing at the Blueberry. It was a reminder of the shells they found in the attic of Bruce Kelly's house—shells from his very beach probably.

She wondered if her mom did this as a girl. She wondered so much about her mom, but in the last few weeks, it had taken a backseat to getting things ready here. Her present took all her time. She didn't have a moment to chase ghosts. But walking on the beach each morning felt like a way she would be close to her mother. The walks unlocked long-ago memories of a fragile woman with a dash of brilliance. Maybe that was the only thing she'd have, those flashes.

Ali turned and walked back towards the cottage. She would have a busy day, which was the way she liked it. Damage control on her failed attempt at hospitality would be at the top of the list. But she found including tasks that she knew she could accomplish and that she could see the results fueled her optimism and spurred her to keep forging ahead with this dream. She could paint rooms. She could clean floors. She could continue to make this place like no place else on earth.

As she walked towards The Sea Turtle she saw a beautiful young blonde woman, hair whipping in the wind. It was unmistakably Katie. She waved. Ali waved back. She was sad that Katie was leaving but also excited about what came next. Katie was almost done with college. Who knew what exciting future would unfurl at her daughter's feet? Her fierce daughter.

Right now, Ali had a dicey mission. She aimed to give her daughter life advice. That was a minefield. She knew. Ali bolstered her will and told herself it was now or never.

"Y'all packed?"

"I'm all packed. I'm surprised how hard it is to leave here," said Katie. That put a smile on Ali's face. She had long-term dreams that included her children and this place. But that had to come here like she did, on their own. Her baby sister was learning this lesson too, that your children became adults and adults had to make their own mistakes, their own decisions.

"Yeah, it turns out it's hard to say goodbye to this beach. I'm unsuccessful at the task."

"I'm mad at you," Katie blurted. It wasn't a joke. Her daughter's emotions were on her face.

"You are?"

"I'm mad at you for leaving us."

And there it was. It was what lay between them lately. There was a huge secret between them, seismic really. Ali decided that she couldn't really share the truth with Katie. What could Ali say to her daughter that wouldn't cause a rift between Ted and Katie or Tye? Telling her children the sordid details about their father was a secret Ali would keep. Even if they hated her for leaving Ted.

"I miss you every day, Katie, but there are reasons that I left, and there are reasons that I didn't come back."

"Mom, Dad does need you."

"Katie, I signed the divorce papers, and so did he. That's done."

"Can you tell me why?"

"Well, you know about his affair." Ali didn't name names. She didn't rehash the dirty details. They knew Ted made one "mistake."

"Yeah, but I want you to forgive him. All midlife crisis men do stupid things. All twenty-something men do stupid things. That's men." Ali hated that her daughter's standard of behavior for the opposite sex was so low.

"Do you want me to forgive him, or do you want me to come back to take care of him?"

"Both."

"Katie, your dad is a good dad." Ali stopped short of anything else. It was true. He was a good dad. He wasn't a good husband. Ali did everything she could to make sure Ted's shortcomings as a husband didn't impact her children's lives.

Did the parents have to have a forever love for the kids to be happy? Ali hoped not because she didn't have it with Ted.

"I want to give you some advice, and of course, I know that at your age, it's hard to accept anything that I might impart." Ali looked out to the water and then back at Katie. Ali told Katie something she'd never learned herself.

"It's not your job to take care of your dad."

"It's easy for you to say, Mom. You're not there."

"I know, and I know he's good at getting people to take care of him, but there's nothing wrong with your dad that he can't take care of himself."

"There's something you're not telling me."

"Your dad and I... failed. Our marriage had nothing to do with you. If I could've stayed longer, I would've. Let's just say there were too many things I could no longer ignore, but you can ignore his pleas that he's unable to do his laundry or can't figure out appointments or needs help with his computer or whatever it is that he's asking you to do. He's a professor for crying out loud! One thing he's said a million times is how smart he is. He's smart enough to take care of himself. If you're smart, you'll let him."

Katie listened. Whether or not she learned, it was her own journey.

"So, I'm kind of thinking I want to come back after graduation."

"I like that idea. And you know I won't miss any of your big events. I'll be there when you walk. I'll be there to help you move wherever you move. I'll be there, and I'll be here. And I answer my texts, you know?"

Katie and Ali hugged. Ali had lied to Katy. She hadn't told her the truth about the extent of the things she could no longer ignore. Maybe she was the bigger person, or maybe she was afraid to open that can of worms. Either way, she felt like she and Katie were in a good place.

Ali hoped that Katie would stop taking care of Ted, but she knew that her own days taking care of Ted Harris were finally and completely over.

Thirty-Eight

FAYE

Sawyer helped Faye load the car.

She was all packed up, and she was tired of hearing everyone's concern about her driving "all that way" alone. Faye reassured her son and her sister that she'd stop in Georgia and then again in Kentucky if she needed to.

And really, she was in no hurry.

She really didn't have a schedule to get back to.

"I'm retired, remember?"

But she didn't feel retired. She felt unmoored. Almost two weeks in Florida had been packed with work, new faces, and the realization that Sawyer wasn't coming back to Ohio with her. But it wasn't packed with a new job or career direction for this old autoworker.

"Remember, don't go to that Deliverance Rest Stop. And keep your head on a swivel, Mom. You are way too confident."

"You could always come on back with me to finish out the semester at UT. Live at home?"

"Mom."

"Kidding."

She'd said goodbye to Didi and Jorge the night before.

Katie and Ted were leaving later. Ted had decamped to a hotel somewhere, but Katie seemed just as torn as Faye did about leaving.

"I'm wondering if the Florida colleges have my program."

"Ahem, they might, but they won't be free tuition," Ali reminded her daughter.

"You're so close to being done. You won't believe how fast your senior year goes. I promise," Faye said. She was reminded again how lucky all their kids were to be able to go to college.

Sawyer and Katie said their goodbyes and then let Ali know their immediate plans.

"We're headed to Rods and Reels to grab breakfast. Need anything, Aunt Ali?"

"I'm good."

Ali and Faye watched their kids walk away.

"Remember when they fought constantly? Something about he's not allowed to play with my America Girl Dolls, and uh, she stole my Charizard card," Faye said.

"I do. Now my girl as a bonus brother, thanks to Sawyer. Makes me very happy to see."

"I know, me too." Sawyer was an only child, but his cousins were nearly as close as siblings. Faye loved that about their family.

"I feel like we were so busy this visit that we didn't visit. You're leaving, and I miss you already."

"I know," Faye said, then sighed. "I, uh, I didn't tell you this because you've got a million plates in the air..."

"What?"

"Blair, I'm worried about Blair."

"Why, is she okay?" Ali was immediately on Big Sister Protective Mode.

"I'm not sure, honestly."

"Is she sick or in danger or what?"

"I don't know. Not sick, but she looked sort of haunted. And I don't think this Blake guy is good for her. At all."

"You need to get her. Get her out of there on your way up."

"I will, or I'll try. There's something else. It feels, somehow, familiar."

Ali cocked her head. "Like how? She's always been so happy-go-lucky and just the lightest of all of us."

That, of course, was because they all treated Blair as the baby she was. Even Bruce Kelly had a soft spot for his youngest girl.

"I know, but it's not her..." Faye didn't finish the sentence.

Ali's face changed. "Is it Mom?"

"You know I have very few memories, but I know you have more. Was Mom...did she have addiction issues?"

Ali looked away, toward the cottages, behind the palms, and out, toward the ocean. It was calm this morning.

"Ali, I may have been little, but I do have some memories. Arguments. Broken glass. 'Mommy has the flu today.'"

Ali put an arm around Faye. She lowered her voice. There was no one around, but it felt like a secret. It felt like something you didn't shout.

"Mom was an alcoholic. I was young too, but you know, I was a thirty-year-old from the jump, right?"

"I know you were the mom most of the time."

"No, she was. She tried to be."

"How much did you protect us from?"

"I think she was very bad off. And the older I got, the worse she got, or the more I understood."

"She was very bad before she died, right? I mean, I remember her being haunted-looking. And that's the part that's scaring me with Blake."

"She was too young to remember any of it. I'm fairly certain of that," Ali said, trying to reassure Faye.

"That's exactly the problem. She's got no memory of how

devastating that disease can be. And yet, she is looking enough like Mom—or what I remember of Mom—that it's got me low-key freaked."

"Can you swing over there on your way home and get eyes on her again?"

"I can. I will."

"Okay, be careful and call me if you're getting tired and after you see Blair and when you get home. Ugh. I wish you both could just move here with me."

"We can't all live the dream. Now, go fix those toilets, get estimates on the foundation stuff for the inn, and make sure Sawyer wears sunscreen. That's on you until my next visit."

They hugged again, and Faye felt sick to her stomach. She didn't want to leave! But she had seeds started at home. She had to find a job.

Faye pulled away from her big sister and fixed in her mind the mission Ali had assigned her.

Find out what was up with Blair.

Find a new career.

Accept that her son was going to be making pottery or something instead of taking economics classes.

It was fine. Everything was fine.

As she pulled onto the highway, Faye had the unsettling feeling that she was leaving home, not driving to it.

Thirty-Nine

DIDI

In the middle of the night, Didi broke out in a cold sweat. At first, she tried not to wake Jorge. Maybe the thermostat of the condo was set too high or too low?

She got up. The pain in her shoulder wasn't getting better either.

She knew getting old was a privilege denied to many, but some days, it was rather tedious. She was standing in the bathroom, staring at the mirror, when things got very gray around the edges of her vision.

"Didi. Didi. Belinda!"

She heard Jorge more than she saw him. He must be mad. He never called her Belinda.

She felt his arms around her as she softly sank to the floor.

"I'm calling an ambulance."

"No, that's ridiculous. I just have a little bug or something."

It was a blur, and at the same time, images registered in her mind. She was in the ambulance. She saw her condo neighbors in every version of pajama you could imagine.

"All these gawkers. I should wave like I'm in a parade."

Jorge held her hand. He also whispered something to the EMTs. They were so cute. Young. Strong.

"I ought to have medical emergencies more often, six young men in my boudoir, heavens!"

"Calm down, Didi. You're going to make things worse."

"Oh Jorge, you're still my favorite."

They gave her medication on the way to the hospital. They put a pressure cuff on her and oxygen in her nose, and in the E.R., she was very popular. People were running around like this was an emergency.

It started to sink in that it *was* an emergency. That *she* was the emergency.

They did tests, and Jorge tried to explain them to her. Time was going too fast and then too slow. It was rush, rush, rush, and wait, wait, wait.

She really hated being in the hospital.

Eventually, hours later, the doctor and Jorge told her the news.

"You've had a heart attack."

"Well, now. I thought it was the flu! How dramatic."

"Didi, this is serious." Jorge looked scared. That scared her, too.

"It was a pretty good heart attack because it showed us something when we did the testing." The doctor was young, too. Was everyone young?

"You have three major blockages, and we're going to need to do surgery to get you better blood flow to that ticker."

"Wait, you're talking bypass surgery?" She was really scared now.

"Yes."

She didn't want to cry, but she felt a tear run down her face.

"When is it scheduled? I'll need an overnight bag. Will you keep me overnight?"

"There isn't really time. And yes, you're going to be here for a little while. This is major surgery."

"You're sure, can't you do—what is it, one of those balloon thingies? My friend Marcine had one of those and she wasn't even overnight."

"Your heart isn't responding to the treatments, so no, that's not going to work. The good news is that the bypass will have you feeling brand new after you recover."

"But you're going to have to crack my chest." She knew this. She'd seen her father have it done. A long time ago, but still.

Didi also knew she could die on the operating table. The doctor spoke with Jorge a little longer, and she tried to stop the panic that was rising. Panic wouldn't be good for her heart! But then they said she was on something, some medicine, to keep her calm.

Great. Okay.

When Jorge came back, she needed to tell him. She needed to get everything off her chest.

"Jorge, I can't die with this secret."

"You're not going to die."

"I very well could. And the girls need to know. I can't keep it from them. And if I go, then you'd have to tell them, and that's not fair."

"That much is true."

"Give me my phone. Did you bring my purse?"

"I did. But you are not calling them right now."

"No, but I'm going to be sure they know. And I'm not leaving it to you or her. This lie can't die with me. It needs to be over."

"Here, point it at me. Do I need lipstick? Oh, heck with it."

"You don't have much time. They said the anesthesiologist is on the way."

"Well, fine. I'll get right to it."

Didi summoned her courage and what was left of her wits.

She looked into the camera phone. And...

Spilled. Her. Guts!

"Ali, Faye, and sweet Blair. I have to tell you something that I've been hiding for most of your lives. It was a secret I helped keep. But not my secret. I did it for your father, he insisted. Yes. I knew Bruce Kelly. I knew him long, long ago when he started dating my sister. My sister's name was Joetta Bennett. My name was Belinda Bennett. So that's part of the secret. I'm your aunt, but that's really not the bombshell."

Didi stopped.

Here it was. She was about to say it out loud. She would have preferred to say it to each of them in person while gathered at The Sea Turtle. She would have preferred not to have to say it at all. It was really her sister's lie. Their father's secret. But Bruce Kelly died before he could tell them.

And at this rate, she might die, too, with this lie. She did not want to show up at the Pearly Gates and explain to St. Peter that she was a dirty, stinking liar.

She needed to tell the truth.

She needed to ask forgiveness. The doctor who was going to put her out was in the doorway.

"Mrs. Rivera, it's time. We need to—"

"Hold on, one second. Anyway, you can hear they're about to send me into surgery. I might not make it. But I want to say I'm sorry. I am so sorry. I just didn't want to lose you girls again. It was too hard the first time. So here it goes. I am your aunt, you heard that, but the real secret I've been keeping is the one I've kept for my sister, your mom. Joetta is my sister, and she is alive. Very much so. Again. I'm sorry. So sorry."

She did cry now; she couldn't help it.

She knew how to send this video to her contacts. She didn't have Blair's contact, but she had Faye and Ali. They were already in a group chat. How convenient.

She sent the video. A little circle appeared in the corner of her phone.

Did it go? Did I do it right?

Another face appeared in the room.

"Belinda! I'm so glad I got here in time, Jorge. She's going to be okay? Right?"

"She's going to be after this surgery."

Didi put the phone down. "God forgive me," she said to St. Peter or whoever was listening in that pre-op room.

Joetta Bennett Kelly Armstrong walked in and kissed her on the head. Didi knew she must be bad off because Joetta was clearly terrified.

She decided to warn Joetta.

"Expect some interesting encounters in the waiting room."

"What?"

"I love you, Sissy. But it's about to get real, as the kids say."

The doctor with the good drugs couldn't wait any longer. He shooed Jorge and Joetta out of the room. If she was lucky, she'd croak on the table, and her sister could finally deal with the fallout of all this.

Didi drifted down, down, down, to a sleep that felt somehow lighter than she'd known in decades.

Amazing what a clear conscious and a dose of Propofol could do.

Forty

FAYE

Faye knocked on the door. She called. She texted. But nothing doing. Blair didn't answer. She'd spent three hours in Cincinnati trying to connect with Blair but had got zero response. She wanted to get home before it got dark.

Where the heck was Blair?

She left a note on the door of Blair's apartment. She sent about a dozen texts, but it was time to get back on the road if she wanted to get home before she fell asleep driving.

After two days behind the wheel, she was cooked, to say the least.

Faye called Ali as she traveled her final leg north on I-75. Faye was getting a little bleary-eyed, so a chat with Ali would keep her alert.

Faye also needed to flesh out something else that had been taking shape in her mind.

"You miss me yet?"

"I do! Oh my gosh, the estimate on roof tiles just came in. I think we're just going to patch, not replace."

"Whatever you think. So, I've had twenty hours to think, and I'm realizing something."

"What?"

Faye hesitated. Was she really considering this? If she said it, there'd be no taking it back. Her sister would go nuts for it. That much Faye was sure of.

"I am realizing I want to turn around and drive twenty hours back!"

"Don't tease me. Really?"

"The weather is getting colder with every mile. With you and now Sawyer there, I am just thinking, maybe I should move down too, just for a little bit."

Once Faye said it out loud, she felt lighter. The gloom she had been encased in since leaving Haven Beach brightened when she voiced her crazy idea.

"That would be perfect!"

Faye hadn't worked out the details, but she didn't have a job to get to in Toledo. She didn't have a son to do laundry for. She didn't have a dad to manage health care appointments for. But maybe more than that, she didn't have her sisters in Toledo anymore.

What she did have was memories of a warm place with new friends and her closest relatives. What if she just called it a sabbatical? She didn't have to decide the rest of her entire life right now. And, who knew, maybe summer would be so hot that she'd come back to Ohio?

"Look," Ali said, in organizer mode. "This is one hundred percent the play. You can stay in one of the cottages or the inn."

"I haven't worked out a single detail. But Rudy even offered me a job at the Grotto." She didn't even want to think about the benefits of seeing Rudy Palmer more often. A man was not the reason she wanted to live in Haven Beach.

"Okay, so rest and regroup. We'll get Blair sorted, and then you need to get back here! I'll get the Lemon ready, or maybe we should work on the Key Lime. Both need work, but I'm putting Sawyer in the little efficiency at the hotel, like we talked about. I want it painted, and he's telling me I don't need to, but you know I'd feel better if it is."

Ali rattled off a million other ideas. Faye was excited. Why not winter in Haven Beach? And spring there, too. She had a smile on her face as nearly an hour of drive time evaporated as they planned.

When they ended the call, Faye was feeling optimistic about her little plan instead of sad to be headed to an empty house.

She still had Blair to worry about, but when Faye arrived home, she was feeling more energized than she should have after all the miles she'd covered.

Faye wasn't ready to sell her little ranch house. She was proud of this place. And she wasn't ready to say she'd leave Toledo forever. But she was ready to stick a toe in the ocean and consider something new. And if she did sell the house, she'd have cash, enough for a while at least. Faye's head was spinning with all the plans, and probably all the coffee she'd consumed on this solo drive.

That's it. Just stick a toe in, Faye Kelly. You can do that much!

Her neighbor had been watering her plants. They looked like they'd survived. Her fridge did smell funky. *Oops.* She'd forgotten to dump out the milk. Faye busied herself with bringing things in from the Jeep and generally opening up her house.

She put her suitcase in her room and avoided looking a Sawyer's. She'd see him soon enough, she realized. Faye wondered how fast she could turn around and get back down to Haven Beach.

For now, she needed to let her neighbor know she was back and thank him for grabbing her mail and watering the plants.

Faye put on her parka and trudged through the snow. She knocked on her next-door neighbor, Mr. Moore's side door. *Dang, it was cold*. Had she gotten spoiled by the beach? Why did the air hurt here?

Mr. Moore flicked on a porch light and answered the door.

"Hey, I'm back. The plants look great. Thank you. I got you a little something as a thank you." Faye knew Mr. Moore loved the Glass City Diner, so she'd gotten him a gift certificate before she'd left. He never wanted her to pay him for watching her place, but he couldn't say no to ham and cheese eggs on her.

"Thanks! It was all good. Oh—I picked up some packages from your porch."

"Oh, gosh, okay. I wasn't expecting anything, but you know how it is? Amazon, am I right?" Faye could easily have forgotten she ordered something. She had a hard time resisting a good lightning deal!

"Uh, and yeah, this too."

Mr. Moore stepped back and opened the door further. He gestured for her to step inside. Faye did so and couldn't believe her eyes.

There, sitting at the kitchen table, roller suitcase next to her, was Blair. Faye also noticed a crate where the famous Darla the Cat lay curled up and snoozing.

"I forgot the garage code," Blair said. "Mr. Moore was this close to giving it to me but wanted to be sure we were actually sisters."

"Blair, I've been trying to get a hold of you or like two days!"

"Yeah, lost my phone. Lost a lot of things."

Faye looked at Mr. Moore, and he shrugged.

"Thanks Mr. Moore, I appreciate you taking in my wayward baby sister. And, not letting a random stranger into my house." This was probably the most excitement her octogenarian neighbor had experienced in months. Mr. Moore simply looked bemused.

Faye walked over to the suitcase, grabbed the handle, and started to roll it to the door.

"Let's go. We have a lot to catch up on."

The two of them slugged through the snow again and back to Faye's little house.

"I don't have food to give you, and well, there's rancid milk if you're thirsty."

"Ha, no worries. I'm not hungry."

Blair still had that haunted look Faye had told Ali about. But at least Blake wasn't there to interrupt or boss Blair.

"So, where's your car?"

"I crashed it."

This made Faye's heart nearly stop. "Oh my gosh, are you okay? Did you total it?"

"Not so much total it as lost my license."

"Wait, why? Was the accident your fault?"

"Yes. No one was hurt. I basically fell asleep at the wheel."

"Honey." Faye hugged Blaire tight. She was so little right now. *What has been going on in her life?*

Blair's red hair, normally a mass of waves and color, hung lifelessly around her shoulders. Her eyes were nearly as red as her hair.

"Okay, so I need to come clean. I am an—I was an—I am an alcoholic."

Faye sat next to Blair and put a hand over her sister's.

"And the accident?"

"Asleep at the wheel, aided by too many cosmos. I was trying to get away from Blake. He is so controlling, you know?"

"I did pick that up," Faye said.

I picked it up, and Sawyer picked it up. You could pick it up from outer space, Faye thought.

"So, I was out, drank more than I realized. Got in the car to drive home and crashed into a ditch. In my head I was pulling over to rest, I guess. But I was asleep, they say that's why I didn't get hurt. I was so relaxed I didn't tense up."

"Thank goodness for that and that you didn't hurt anyone else."

"Right. So, I went to AA right away. I pled guilty right away, too. No one was hurt. No damage to property. And I said I was sorry. I am sorry. And I'm determined. With Blake out of the picture, I can do this."

"I know you can."

"I have a little cash saved, but I have to tell you something awful."

"It's all awful, and this has been going on when we were in Florida?"

"Yeah, rough two weeks on my end. Anyway. Blake wasn't there for any of it."

"What a jerk."

"So, here it goes. He sold Mommy's pearls and kept the money." Blair said it like someone had been murdered. "He snatched them out of the box and pawned them! I tried to get them back, but they were gone." She wiped a tear that threatened to spill out of her left eye.

Faye thought Blair looked exactly like she did when she was a little girl at that moment.

"He's put all these ultimatums down. I just snapped. I got my suitcase and walked out. I had my phone and called the Uber to the bus station. But I left my phone. Which was very stupid. But I wasn't in my right mind, you know?"

"No wonder I couldn't get a hold of you."

"Yeah, he still has my phone. I don't think he has the passcode, so I should be fine. The main thing is I got Darla out of there." She opened the cat's little door, but Darla decided to stay in the crate.

Probably smart since the poor thing had never been to Faye's. Faye looked at the little kitty and then back to her baby sister. At that moment, Blair completely fell apart. She started sobbing, her body racked with emotion.

Faye didn't say anything. She just dropped down to the floor with her sister and held Blair until it all came out.

"Honey, why didn't you tell us? We could have helped."

"You're both so together. And I was falling apart, a total loser."

"Alcoholism isn't being a loser; it's a disease you have, and one I recently learned Mommy had too. It is in no way your fault."

Blair let out a sigh. "So, here's the thing. Blake is uh, angry, and I'm uh, well, in the hospital after the crash they found out that I'm, uh, pregnant."

Faye waited for a beat.

She wanted Blair to have her own feelings about that. She didn't want to celebrate if the celebration was the last thing on her sister's mind.

"And how do you feel about that?"

"I'm scared. I'm scared about all of it. I thought I was infertile. I tried and tried, and now boom, worst frigging timing. I'm practically geriatric in pregnancy terms."

"You're not alone. You have me, and Ali, and we'll get this sorted with you. However, you want."

"I don't want to tell Blake right now. He's not going to be a good dad. I mean, I don't think I'm going to be a good mom either, but he for sure would suck as a dad. I'm an almost forty-year-old unwed mother. I'm really doing things backward."

"We don't have to decide all of this right now. We just have to take one step at a time."

Darla was a light brown kitty with a little, white-tipped tail. Seeing Blair break down prompted Darla finally to pad out of the crate. She wound herself around Blair's leg.

Faye hadn't even unpacked. Her phone was dead. The milk was bad. But her sister was here, and her seedlings had survived.

They'd figure out the rest of it, one crisis at a time.

She was going to be an aunt again!

That was amazing, no matter what the circumstance.

Forty-One

ALI

As messages went, this one was ridiculous. It was Didi, clearly in the hospital, clearly looking very gray, clearly spelling something out that made zero sense. Her words were about as clear as mud.

Didi was going in for heart surgery. That was part one. Part two, the unburdening of a secret so preposterous that it seemed a product of medication or fabrication, not the actual truth.

Ali replayed the message ten times. She called Didi's phone.

No answer. She was probably in surgery now if the first part of the message was right.

What hospital? Was she delusional? What the heck?

She needed answers. Okay, Jorge, she'd call Jorge.

It felt like she was losing her mind. Was she the one having a stroke?

Finally, Jorge answered his phone.

Ali wanted to bombard him with the big question. Still, first, before anything else, she asked about how they were doing.

"She is in her third hour of surgery. I am holding up. But I imagine that's not the question you really want to ask."

"No, so you saw the message?"

"I did."

"Is she hallucinating?

"No."

"Did you know she's been lying? I can't believe anything she's said up to now. How in the world can I?"

"I wish I could offer you more, but here is where I am. My wife, who I love the most of anyone on this planet, might die today. At that moment, she decided she wanted to be sure you knew, if she died, what she had done. But I don't have it in me to comfort you when I am feeling very—"

Jorge broke down.

She loved Jorge and Didi. What he said cut to the quick. She knew what it was like to lose someone forever. Her father's death was fresh in her mind.

"What hospital?"

"I need you to promise you will not cause a scene if she survives it." Jorge was the protector now, and Ali knew he would protect Didi.

"I promise."

"Tampa General."

"Be there in an hour. I am coming for you and her and not to make any scene."

They ended the call.

And that was true. Yes, she could not believe any of what Didi had said. Aunt Didi? Her mother, alive? This was all completely insane. But the only way she'd get answers is if Didi got better. So, she'd be there to support Jorge and then maybe she'd find out what exactly Didi was talking about.

At that point, Ali realized Faye was also on the group text. She needed to talk to Faye. Ali could not imagine how Faye was taking this bomb Didi had dropped.

She called Faye and Blair. No answer. She texted them to call. No answer.

Finally, she left her own messages on their voicemail.

"I need you to meet me at Tampa General. If you saw the message I just saw, we need answers. Get to Florida, okay? Full stop, like 911. This is more than I can handle alone."

And there it was. Ali needed help. She needed her sisters.

Didi was their aunt, and their mother was alive?

The words her father said to her on his deathbed came back to her.

She saw him in her memory, struggling to say something in his last hours, his last minutes.

"I did it to keep you three safe."

"You could have died." (Who could have died?)

"I tried to do my best. But I'm not her." (Ali had believed her father was hallucinating, seeing their long-gone mother, maybe?)

"It had to be done. Cut off. The only way."

"I thought—I'm sorry—Tell Faye and Blair."

Cut off. That's what he said. Who was cut off?

Is that what he meant? Their mother was alive, and he was a part of the lie?

The lie that changed their lives forever.

How could a woman leave her children? Why? Ali thought of Tye and Katie. She couldn't imagine a reason or scenario that would have her leaving them, that would make her stay away for their entire lives.

Where were her sisters? Why didn't they answer their phones?

Ali's own heart rate was going to head to cardiac arrest levels with all this earth-shattering information.

She realized she was spiraling. She took a breath.

Then she found Sawyer.

"Sawyer, Didi is in the hospital. I'm going to go visit. Can you hold down the fort here?"

"No guests, yeah, I think I can handle it. Is it serious with Miss Didi?"

"Yes."

"Is she going to be okay?"

"I don't know, but if your mom calls, tell her to get herself to the hospital. Tampa General."

"What, wait, she barely got home. She's coming back?"

"I'll bet a million dollars on that one, yes. And for longer than you'd guess."

Sawyer shook his head like there was something in his ears. "Okay, what else?"

"That's it. I'm heading out in a minute. Just, thank you. I appreciate your help."

"No problem, Aunt Ali. Glad I am here."

"I am, too; you're a great help."

Ali got in her car and tried to obey all traffic laws on her race to Tampa General.

She had no idea what she would find once she got there.

Forty-Two

BLAIR

Faye handled everything. Darla's transport. Their tickets. She said it wasn't much to pack and button up the house since it was never unbuttoned from her last trip to Florida.

This time, they were flying.

They'd gone to bed and around 6 a.m.

Faye woke her up, looking serious. "I need you to sort of brace yourself. I have a message here from the woman who's been the manager of The Sea Turtle."

"Didi?"

"Yes."

Blair hadn't met Didi, but she'd listened to Faye and Ali's stories about The Sea Turtle. She could picture Didi and Jorge. She could imagine the salty air. It all seemed so fun. She would otherwise be very excited to head down, but the message Faye played was completely and utterly bonkers.

"She's our aunt?

"I think she's having a psychotic break or something, or I did,

210

and then Ali left me a message that we need to get down there. Like right now."

"But can we?"

"This was a 911 deal on Ali's part. She needs us, and we go, got it?"

"Yes, I do. I'm already packed."

"Yep, flights out of Eugene Krantz at 9 a.m."

"Okay, let's get going."

Blair hadn't had a drink in over ten days. And honestly, she felt great. Somehow, dealing with this was better than dealing with Blake. She felt clear-headed, if not a little tired, thanks to the pregnancy she supposed. But whatever the case, Ali was in need. Their big sister never asked for help, so if she needed something, it was important.

It did not register that anything this Didi said could be true.

Their mother was long gone. Blair had almost no memory of her. She told herself she had it the best of the three Kelly Sisters in that department. Blair couldn't miss what she never had.

Faye's mother-henned her all the way to the plane and through the airport and to a rental car. Blair even napped with Darla on her lap on the ride from St. Pete Airport to the hospital.

When they got to the parking garage, who should appear but her handsome nephew. Another detail Faye had handled.

"I'll take Darla to The Sea Turtle, and you get there when you get there."

Sawyer hugged his mom and his aunt, and Faye turned to her.

"You ready for this?"

"I have no idea what all this is."

"Me either, really."

The sisters made their way up to the floor where Didi Rivera was in recovery.

They walked down the halls, and finally, they found Ali. She looked slightly mental. Her blonde hair was a mess when it was usually nicely smoothed and styled. Her face was free of makeup. But her eyes were lined with dark circles.

It was good to see her, nonetheless. The three sisters hugged. They didn't say anything for a moment. Blair had so many questions. But she was late to the party. This Didi person was a stranger to her. Still, somehow, that message had her sisters flying across the country and showing up with no makeup in public. It was serious. Whatever it was.

"Let's go see Didi," Faye said.

"Okay," Ali agreed, "but I promised Jorge we won't upset her."

"Who is Jorge?" Blair asked.

"Didi's husband."

"So, our uncle, if Didi is to be believed," Blair pointed out.

Ali shrugged.

They walked together, a band of three, into the hospital room of a woman who was looking so very little but alive. Blair could see the monitor blinking a heartbeat and a blood pressure that was in the range of normal.

Didi turned to see the three Kelly Sisters.

"Oh, Baby Blair! I wanted to meet you so badly. Not like this, but I think about you every day."

A man sat next to the bed; this must be Jorge. He patted his wife's hand.

"How are you, Didi?" Ali asked.

"Been better, but they tell me I've been worse. The surgery worked. So that's the good news. Don't you have a more important question?"

The woman's voice was so weak. *This was a lot, whatever it was*, Blair thought.

"We don't want to upset you, just rest," Ali said.

"Oh, okay. But uh, oh boy."

Jorge and Didi looked beyond the Kelly Sisters. Blair followed their gaze.

A new person had entered the room.

She was blonde, petite, and if Blair didn't have Ali's hand in hers, she'd have sworn it was Ali with an age filter on.

No one said a word.

The woman stood as tall as she could.

"My name is Joetta Armstrong, and I'm your mother."

The monitor attached to Didi started beeping. Her heart rate spiked.

Blair figured that if she had on a blood pressure monitor too, hers would be doing the exact same thing.

Forty-Three

JOETTA

She knew they would hate her. They should hate her. She hated herself.

Joetta stared at the three beautiful women in front of her. They held hands tightly. They were a force together.

She wanted that for them. She wanted everything for them.

Joetta had spied on her children over the years. In the early days, it was difficult. But now, thanks to Facebook, she'd see glimpses of them all.

What did the kids call it? Lurking? She'd lurked on the periphery of their social media.

It was easy to track down Ali, so like her. Ali was her mini back in the day and really still was.

Faye looked more like Bruce, handsome Bruce. Faye's hair was chestnut like Bruce's was.

And Baby Blair. Her sweet redhead.

Joetta corrected herself. She had no right to call these three hers. They had made their way in the world without her.

They were the Kelly Sisters, not the Gulfside Girls like her and Didi.

Didi had finally spilled the beans. She'd threatened to tell in the early days. But over the years, the lie became easier to forget. This was just the way it was. The decade she'd spent in Toledo was a fever dream.

It was this life with Banks that was her real life.

But there was no denying it now. In fact, looking at Ali in particular meant none of them could deny it. These were her three daughters.

Three daughters that Bruce had done everything he could to keep from her. At first, she'd fought for the right to see them. But that was short-lived.

And now Bruce was gone. Didi was clinging to life. And her three girls were in front of her. Not one had a smile on their face.

Joetta didn't have any words other than introducing herself.

And inside, the words *I'm sorry* replayed on a loop. *I'm sorry. I'm sorry. I'm sorry.* But she didn't say it.

She was about to try to explain, to let them ask her questions.

But the monitor attached to her sister was beeping louder and louder.

Jorge stood up and pressed the call button.

Two nurses came in. They were in a frenzy around Didi.

Joetta sent up a prayer. *Please let her be okay.* She needed her big sister if she was going to face the truth of what she'd done.

The Gulfside Girls would need each other to face the Kelly Sisters and the questions they surely had every right to ask.

The Gulfside Girls and Kelly Sisters Saga Continues in the next book of the Haven Beach Novels - Gulfside Secret!

Also by Rebecca Regnier

Summer Cottage Novels

- Sandbar Sisters
- Sandbar Season
- Sandbar Summer
- Sandbar Storm
- Sandbar Sunrise

Haven Beach Beachy Women's Fiction Series

- Gulfside Girls
- Gulfside Inn
- Gulfside Secret
- Gulfside Wish
- Gulfsdie Sunset

About the Author

Rebecca Regnier is an award-winning newspaper columnist, tv host, and former television news anchor. She lives in Michigan with her family and handsome dog. For all the latest from the beach and an exclusive bonus scene sign up for her newsletter or follow her on one of her socials. She loves to share laughs with her readers!

tiktok.com/@rebeccaregnier

facebook.com/rlregnier

instagram.com/rebeccaregnier

youtube.com/@RebeccaRegnierTV

Made in the USA
Monee, IL
11 May 2025